Blake lifted Jessie easily from the saddle and swung her down beside him. Still holding her around the waist, he said, "I think that's the way they used to do it in the movies."

"You're right." She felt a rush of heat as she looked up at him. "Except you left out the best part."

Without thinking she lifted her lips to his. He needed no further invitation. The kiss started as a brief, pleasurable exchange between friends, but as his lips moved across hers it grew to unbridled passion. Automatically her arms encircled his neck, her fingers caressing his hair.

He pulled her close against him, deepening the kiss. She felt the muscled strength of him, pressed against the wide expanse of his chest. She kissed him mindlessly, letting go of all her caution, seizing the moment without thinking of the consequences.

"Jessie," he murmured against her lips. "Beautiful Jessie."

"Don't stop." The words were a broken plea. "I don't want you to stop."

His arms tightened around her, and there was no mistaking his desire. All the pent-up passion, all the long-hidden need, came rushing to the surface. And this time, neither of them tried to deny it . . .

WHAT ARE *LOVESWEPT* ROMANCES?

They are stories of true romance and touching emotion. We believe those two very important ingredients are constants in our highly sensual and very believable stories in the *LOVESWEPT* line. Our goal is to give you, the reader, stories of consistently high quality that may sometimes make you laugh, sometimes make you cry, but are always fresh and creative and contain many delightful surprises within their pages.

Most romance fans read an enormous number of books. Those they truly love, they keep. Others may be traded with friends and soon forgotten. We hope that each *LOVESWEPT* romance will be a treasure—a "keeper." We will always try to publish

LOVE STORIES YOU'LL NEVER FORGET
BY AUTHORS YOU'LL ALWAYS REMEMBER

The Editors

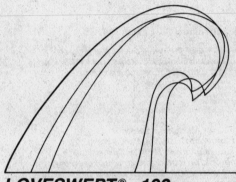

LOVESWEPT® • 192

Peggy Webb
The Joy Bus

 BANTAM BOOKS
TORONTO • NEW YORK • LONDON • SYDNEY • AUCKLAND

THE JOY BUS

A Bantam Book / May 1987

LOVESWEPT® *and the wave device are registered*
trademarks of Bantam Books, Inc. Registered in U.S. Patent
and Trademark Office and elsewhere.

If you would be interested in receiving protective vinyl
covers for your Loveswept books, please write to this address
for information:

Loveswept
Bantam Books
P.O. Box 985
Hicksville, NY 11802

ISBN 0-553-21813-1

Published simultaneously in the United States and Canada

Bantam Books are published by Bantam Books, Inc. Its trademark, consisting of the words "Bantam Books" and the por-
trayal of a rooster, is Registered in U.S. Patent and Trademark
Office and in other countries. Marca Registrada. Bantam
Books, Inc., 666 Fifth Avenue, New York, New York 10103.

PRINTED IN THE UNITED STATES OF AMERICA

O   0 9 8 7 6 5 4 3 2 1

One

Jessie whipped her Ferrari down the curving driveway, oblivious to the fog. She drove the way she did everything else, with reckless ease. Suddenly, an object loomed in her path.

"Good grief! A pink bus," she said as she slammed on her brakes, slewing her car sideways and stopping a hair's breadth from the bus.

She peered through the fog to assure herself that the pink bus wasn't a mirage. It wasn't. It was parked right in the middle of her driveway, an ancient school bus, pinker than cotton candy. Foot high letters in garish purple proclaimed it The Joy Bus.

Jessie barreled out of her car, pulling her Russian sable coat close around her neck against the January chill, and marched forward to find out what sort of idiot drove a pink bus and why it was parked in her way. And on a foggy morning, to boot, she fumed. It was a wonder she hadn't broken her neck, and then where would Wentworth Enterprises be?

Through the patchy fog, she saw a man emerge from under the hood of the bus.

"Do you always drive like that?" he asked.

His question got her dander up immediately. She strode toward him as she talked. "Do you always park in the middle of the road on foggy mornings? You almost got us both killed."

She was now standing directly in front of him, close enough to see that he was tall, well built, good looking, and probably on the right side of forty. He was so tall, in fact, that he might have been intimidating to anybody else, but Jessie Wentworth was five nine. There were very few people she couldn't look in the eye, and nobody intimidated her.

"I asked you the first question," he said.

"How I drive is none of your business."

Unexpectedly, the man smiled. "You're right." He pushed his knit cap back from his forehead. "This conversation seems to have gotten off to a bad start. Let's start over." He extended his hand. "I'm Blake Montgomery."

"Jessie Wentworth."

She had put her hand in his and answered automatically. She was thankful that she had been well trained in southern manners, otherwise she might have stood in the middle of the road and stared at his hair. When he had pushed his cap back, a shock of bright hair had fallen forward. Even in the fog, she could see that it was the color of freshly mown wheat. Nobody in her family had hair like that. The Wentworths were all blessed with hair as black as doom, a heritage from some Indian ancestors.

"My noble vehicle," he said, "began gasping for breath a few miles from here. Fortunately, I was able to pull it off the road and onto your driveway before it died."

He smiled again. Jessie figured it was one of the most engaging smiles she had ever seen. He was probably a con artist, she thought. She pulled her hand out of his and shoved it into her coat pocket.

"How long do you think it will take you to fix it?" she asked. "I'm on my way to work."

"With a little luck, not long. I'm accustomed to all her idiosyncrasies. Why don't you hop inside to wait? It's cold out here. Only be careful not to sit on the rabbits."

"Rabbits! I'd as soon wait in a pit of alligators."

"You don't like rabbits?"

"I hate them. They're all vicious little creatures trying to fool everybody with their cute Easter bunny faces. I'll wait in my car, thank you." She started to leave, then turned back for a last word. "Do try to hurry."

Blake watched her walk to her car. What kind of woman went to work wearing a fur coat and driving a Ferrari? he wondered. She was beautiful enough to be a high fashion model. That was probably it. Somebody spoiled and pampered, somebody used to having the whole world groveling at her feet.

He turned his attention back to the bus. No use speculating about the aristocratic Jessie Wentworth, he decided. He would have The Joy Bus going in no time flat and be on his way to places unknown. He'd never see Jessie Wentworth again. A pity. He found her fascinating. He wondered why she didn't like rabbits.

Jessie, snug once more in her car, picked up the car phone and called her office.

"I'll be late this morning, Clarice," she told her secretary. "Do I have any appointments scheduled?"

She could hear Clarice flipping through the appointment book.

"None, Miss Wentworth. Hunter Chadwick's secretary called to confirm that he's on his way to Jackson. He arrives on the six o'clock plane."

"Call Raymond and have him meet Hunter at the airport. He's to bring him directly to Wentworth Manor."

"Yes, ma'am. Anything else?"

Jessie smiled. She didn't know why Clarice Gibbs always called her ma'am. She was Clarice's junior by a good twenty years.

"Tell Helga I want to see the portfolio on the new lingerie designs today, and if Marcus Formby calls, set up an appointment for this afternoon. I'm definitely interested in his line of designer chocolates."

Having completed her business, Jessie settled back and watched Blake Montgomery. The fog was beginning to lift, so she had a better view of him. He was much handsomer than she had first thought. She figured all con artists were handsome. It would be a definite asset to their operations or whatever they called their work.

She tapped her polished nails on the dashboard. Inactivity didn't suit Jessie Wentworth. She had been involved in the running of Wentworth Enterprises almost since she was big enough to sit on her father's knee at the board meetings. He had turned the management of the Wentworth department stores over to Jessie on her twenty-first birthday. She had confirmed his faith in her by doubling the number of stores in the last eight years. The latest Wentworths had opened in Dallas last week.

When her parents returned from Sweden, the first thing she wanted to do was fly out to Dallas with them and show them the new store.

Her fingernails continued their impatient rat-a-tatting in the quiet car as she waited for the con artist to get his joy bus going again. She studied the garish lettering on the side of the bus. What kind of man drove a joy bus? she wondered. Was it a clever ruse to cover his activities? Was he like a rabbit, hiding his viciousness behind a cute facade?

At the thought of rabbits, a scene from her childhood sprang into her mind. She remembered the fresh colors and the smells of spring—the sunset pink of the rosebuds, the tender green of the grass, the sweet perfume of the narcissus. She rubbed her hands over her eyes. Lord, she would never forgive that rabbit.

She glanced at her watch with irritation. What was taking that man so long? He was going to freeze. Not that she cared. Well, maybe some, she amended. She'd hate to see that beautiful hair go to waste.

She stepped out of her car and approached the man again.

"Aren't you finished yet?" she asked.

"I'm afraid not. It looks as if I'm going to have to call a mechanic."

Jessie hesitated only a moment before she made her decision. She thought she was a pretty good judge of people, and while Blake Montgomery was probably a con artist, he appeared to be a harmless one. Nobody with hair the color of wheat and gray eyes framed with smile lines could be a kidnapper.

"I'll have my mechanic tow your bus to our

garage," she said. "You can wait at the house until repairs are made."

"Does that generous offer include hot coffee?"

"Yes. Mrs. Jones will take care of your needs."

Blake was vaguely disappointed. Although Jessie Wentworth had said she was on her way to work, he had hoped for a small visit. One just long enough to peel back a layer or two of her personality and see if she were really as fascinating as he had first thought. It was her remark about rabbits that intrigued him the most.

Jessie walked back toward her car. "I'll take you up to the house."

"Wait. First I have to get the animals."

Before she could protest, he bounded aboard The Joy Bus, emerging a few minutes later with his pockets bulging and a small bundle of fur tucked under his arm. The bundle of fur growled at Jessie as he got into the Ferrari.

He patted the small dog's head. "This is Sandy."

Sandy acknowledged the introduction by baring her teeth at Jessie in a snarl that would have been vicious if she had weighed sixty pounds instead of five.

"That dog hates me," Jessie said. She backed the Ferrari away form the pink bus and expertly manipulated a turn that would take them to the house.

"Nonsense," Blake said. "Sandy loves everybody."

Sandy made him a liar by taking a quick nip at Jessie's Russian sable coat.

"It must be the coat," he said.

He muzzled Sandy with his hand and settled back for the hair-raising ride up the winding driveway.

"Do you ever dent one of these trees?" he asked.

"Never. My driving teacher was a man who used to race in the Grand Prix."

"That figures." Blake held his breath as they rounded a sharp curve. On two wheels, he speculated.

It was either the heat or the wild driving that brought the rabbits out of hiding. First, their pink-lined ears emerged from Blake's coat pockets, then their curious little noses became visible.

Jessie nearly wrecked the car. "Rabbits," she yelled. She wrestled with the steering wheel and got back on her hell-bent-for-leather course.

When Blake's heart moved out of his mouth, he said, "They're a part of my act and are perfectly harmless. George hasn't snarled at anybody since he was born, and Floyd wouldn't say boo if a grizzly bear had him by the ears."

As if on cue, the doves in Blake's inside coat pockets cooed. The Ferrari made another erratic swipe at the trees. Once again, Jessie brought it under control.

"I thought you said he wouldn't say boo."

"That wasn't the rabbits; that was the doves."

"The doves? My Lord, who are you?"

"A magician by avocation; a professor of psychology by profession. I'm on sabbatical from the University of Mississippi."

Jessie laughed. "I thought you were a con artist."

"The pink bus confuses a lot of people."

"No, it was your smile." She braked the car to a stop. "We're home."

Blake stared out the window. "Home" was a huge mansion styled after the antebellum showplaces that had been razed during the Civil War. The white columns and wide verandas might have been straight out of *Gone With the Wind*. It all

fit, he thought. The coat, the car, the house. Jessie Wentworth was wealthy.

"Come in," she said. "I'll introduce you to Mrs.
Jones."

"The one with the hot coffee?"

"Yes."

They got out of the car and started toward the
house. Blake put Sandy down to follow along behind and fell into step beside Jessie. Too close
beside her, for one of the rabbits stuck his head
out of Blake's pocket again. His silky ears rubbed
against Jessie's hand. She jumped away so fast
that she lost her balance.

Blake steadied her by grabbing her arm. She
stared up at him, and he was mesmerized by her
green eyes. They were heavily lashed, exotic, slightly
slanted, and at the moment, wide with fright. He
felt a compelling urge to kiss her eyelids and murmur soothing words into her ear. He released her
arm reluctantly, wishing he had some reason to
keep holding it.

Jessie was transfixed. Her heart was doing the
two-step against her ribcage, but it was more than
fright. It was the closeness of this man, this magician with animals in his pockets. Was he prac-
ticing magic on her now? she wondered. How else
could she explain her reaction?

"There now," he said. He wanted to reach out
and smooth her hair as one would when comforting a child. Instead he smiled. He had no earthly
idea why he felt all these protective urges toward
a woman who was obviously self-sufficient. "You're
safe."

But she wasn't, Jessie thought. As long as she
felt this way standing close to him, she wasn't
safe. She widened the distance between them and
made a sound that she hoped passed for laughter.

"Of course, I'm safe." Brave words from a not-so-brave woman. "It's just that I have a silly fixation about rabbits. Please tell Floyd to keep his nose in your pocket."

"That was George."

"Well, whoever he is, tell him to keep his bunny nose out of my way."

Blake patted the rabbit's head. "You heard that, George. No more stunts on your own. You'll have to wait for the black top hat."

Jessie led him through her front door. "You have a black top hat?"

"Standard issue for magicians."

"What about the pink bus? Is that also standard issue?"

"No. The bus is special."

He didn't elaborate and she didn't ask him to. She pressed an intercom button and spoke first to her mechanic, then to her housekeeper.

The professor of magic stood in the opulent hallway, admiring the house. It was a beautiful setting for a beautiful woman, he decided. A curving rosewood staircase led upward to a chandelier of Austrian crystal, whose prisms cast a rainbow across the gallery of portraits lining the wall alongside the stairs. The Wentworth ancestors looked back at him from their gilt-edged frames. If they could have talked, they would probably have asked what manner of man Jessie had brought to the estate.

As Jessie turned from the intercom, she was wondering the same thing. Blake Montgomery didn't fall into any of the categories she had reserved for men. He was neither too eager, too obsequious, nor too sly. He was self-possessed, dignified, and charming, if you forgot about the rabbits in his pockets.

She was saved further speculation by the entrance of her housekeeper. Mrs. Jones was a tall, raw-boned woman with a forbidding face and a marshmallow heart. Her dark hair, streaked with silver, was woven into braids and wrapped around her head. It gave the impression that she was wearing a crown; and she might have been, for she ruled absolute in the Wentworth household.

"Mrs. Jones," Jessie said, "this is Dr. Blake Montgomery. He'll be staying here until his bus is repaired. Will you see that he has everything he needs?"

Mrs. Jones studied the visitor from head to toe. Her sharp eyes didn't miss a thing, most certainly not the animals.

"Did you bring your own dinner?" she asked. "I don't think the cook knows how to prepare rabbit stew."

Blake roared with laughter. "Don't let George and Floyd hear you say that. They're liable to resign from my magic act."

The instant he said "magic" he won Mrs. Jones's heart. She had eight grandchildren, and her greatest joy was in taking them to every circus and magic show that came to town.

"Jessie, it looks like you've finally brought home a man we can trust."

"Mrs. Jones," Jessie said warningly, but the housekeeper was not deterred. Nothing ever stopped her from speaking her piece.

"If you can't trust a magician, who can you trust?" Mrs. Jones continued. "Anybody who makes children happy is welcome in the Wentworth household."

"He'll be staying only a short while," Jessie said. "Alvin is repairing his bus. In the meantime, I think he could use a cup of coffee."

As Mrs. Jones left to get the coffee, Blake turned to Jessie.

"Off to work?" he asked.

"Yes."

"Then I probably won't see you again."

"Probably not." Jessie was appalled at herself. She seemed suddenly to have forgotten the art of conversation. Blake was having the same trouble.

"Thank you for coming to my rescue," he said. "A man could freeze on a day like this." His tiny mop of a dog scrunched up against his legs and snarled at Jessie. "Sandy, too. Although she doesn't seem to appreciate it."

It was the dog that brought Jessie to her senses. "I must be going now. If you need anything, Mrs. Jones will take care of you."

"Indeed, I will," Mrs. Jones said, rejoining them. "I've arranged for cake and hot coffee upstairs in my apartment." She waved her hand toward Jessie. "Scoot along to that store of yours. I'll take good care of your man." Mrs. Jones took Blake's arm and led him toward the staircase.

He turned toward Jessie and gave her a quick wink before he was hustled up the stairs. Jessie felt a small sense of deprivation as they disappeared. Mrs. Jones's voice drifted down to her. "Doctor, did you say? I have this pain under my ribs . . . What kind of doctor does magic? We'll have to hide these rabbits—and, my Lord! birds! —from the cook. She's crabby." Her words faded away as she and Blake were swallowed up by the cavernous upstairs.

Jessie stood in the entry hall smiling. Dr. Blake Montgomery would certainly not be lonely while he waited. Mrs. Jones talked a mile a minute and would regale him with every tale in her repertoire, from the tragedy of her last operation to the comedy of her romance with the governor's security guard.

Jessie had the sudden feeling that she would be missing something wonderful if she left now. She wanted to toss her sable coat across the banister and follow them up the stairs. She wanted to sit in Mrs. Jones's apartment and watch the man she had rescued. She wanted to memorize the look of his fine hair and record the sound of his voice. She wanted to find out why his bus was painted pink and why it had that intriguing name—The Joy Bus. Did the professor know something about life that she didn't? She would never find out. He would be gone by the time she returned from work.

She toyed with the idea of staying home, but dismissed it almost immediately. She'd had too many disappointments with men before. They all seemed to be after one thing—her money. As she walked out the door, leaving Blake Montgomery behind, she rationalized that she didn't want to find out the hard way that the magic man with the wheat-colored hair was just a con artist after all.

After waving to Alvin, who had towed the pink bus up to the garage, Jessie climbed into her car and roared off down the winding lane. The fog had completely lifted, and all the trees that she had narrowly missed on her perilous journey back to the house were in full view. She laughed in exultation as she whizzed by the massive oaks and ancient magnolias and shot onto the road, headed for downtown Jackson.

She parked her car in the underground garage of Wentworths department store and took the private elevator to her suite of offices on the top floor. The offices were starkly modern with lots of windows and open space. A Henri Matisse oil dominated one wall, and an abstract bronze by Alberto Giacometti presided over the sitting area located under a group of skylights.

Jessie almost always paused to admire the Giacometti sculpture, but today was different. She breezed by it with scarcely a glance. Saying a quick "good morning" to her secretary, she entered her private office. Seated behind her desk, Jessie picked up her morning mail. She had to go through it four times before it made any sense. By the time she had finished that chore, she was thoroughly hot and bothered. And then she realized she was still wearing her fur coat.

Impatiently she cast the coat aside and picked up the design portfolio she had told Clarice to have ready. The lingerie designs by one of Wentworth's top couturiers were new and exciting, but they failed to claim Jessie's attention. Wheat-colored hair and crystal gray eyes kept getting in the way. She finally put the designs down in disgust.

"This is ridiculous," she said aloud. "I've got to stop thinking about that magician."

But she could not. She thought about the way his hand had felt on hers and the way he had looked when he smiled. She thought about his pink bus and his pocketful of doves. She even thought about his rabbits.

She wondered what it would be like to have a relationship with a man like that, and then she wondered if all his charm and sincerity were a facade. If she could see him again, she might find out. She toyed with the idea of calling Alvin and instructing him to postpone the bus repair until tomorrow. She never backed down at rearranging fate, but today something stopped her. What right did she have to hold him practically hostage just to satisfy her curiosity? she asked herself. The best thing to do would be to forget him.

But Jessie Wentworth, who could run a huge corporation with the greatest of ease, couldn't forget the man who was magic.

Two

Blake ate the last crumb of the best cake he had ever tasted—blueberry jam cake, Mrs. Jones had said—and tried to keep track of the woman's hop-scotch conversation.

"I've been with the Wentworth family for twenty years. Did I tell you that?" She had. Three times already. But he didn't tell her so. "Since Jessie was a little girl. A spunky little thing, she was. Still is. And works like a man. She's her daddy's pride and joy. Of course, I have a few myself. Pride and joys, that is. Eight grandchildren. I almost landed them a new grandfather a while back. The governor's security guard. If it hadn't been for that guard dog, we'd still be courting. One night. . ."

Blake grinned as she launched into the story of her courtship for the second time. He gave the appearance of listening to her, but actually he was thinking about Jessie Wentworth. Mrs. Jones had been right; she was spunky. Lively and inde-pendent, too. He liked that in a woman. He hoped his bus wouldn't be repaired until after she returned from work.

"Here, let me cut you another piece of cake." Mrs. Jones reached for his plate and refilled it before he could protest. "A big man like you needs lots of food. You need a wife, too. Why don't you have a wife?"

Blake laughed at her boldness. People never ceased to fascinate him. "It's no secret. I don't have a wife because I've never met a woman I wanted to share my life with."

"Bosh! A handsome man like you? I'll bet that university you told me about is crawling with women itching to get into your pants."

He almost choked on his cake. He figured that he had never met a more forward woman than the Wentworth housekeeper.

Mrs. Jones laughed. "You didn't expect me to say that, did you? I decided when I reached the age of forty I was old enough to say exactly what I wanted to without bothering what other people thought. By the time you reach forty, you either have friends or you don't, and what you say isn't going to make a whole hell of a lot of difference. Unless you say things to hurt, of course. If I have a mean remark, I try to keep it to myself."

"That's an intriguing philosophy."

"I never thought of it as philosophy. It's just the way I am."

"I admire a person who knows himself."

"Jessie does."

"Does what?"

"Knows herself. Only trouble is, she doesn't trust men. She's been engaged before, did I tell you?"

Blake leaned forward in his chair. Whether the Wentworth housekeeper should be telling family secrets or not didn't bother him. He was gleaning another bit of information to add to the puzzle of Jessie.

"No, you didn't," he said.

"He was a fine-looking man, big and athletic, sort of like you in that respect. Rich, too. Or so we all thought. I guess that's one reason Jessie fell for him. She didn't think he would be marrying her for her money. She found out the hard way that that's exactly what he was doing. She overheard a conversation in the powder room at the country club. He was going to use her money to rebuild his sagging family business. Besides that, he was seeing another woman the whole time they were engaged."

"She must have been devastated."

"Not so you would notice. Jessie always tries to keep a stiff upper lip. But it hurt. I could tell. I know her as well as I do my own child. She tries hard to be tough, but she's really a little girl inside."

Blake could have stayed the rest of the day learning about Jessie and enjoying the outrageous company of Mrs. Jones, but Alvin soon sent word that The Joy Bus was ready to travel. Blake thanked Mrs. Jones for her hospitality, gathered his contented animals off her hearth rug, and went to the garage to pick up his bus.

He loaded his menagerie and headed south on Interstate 55. He whistled a merry tune as he drove, happy to be on the road again, content to be combining work with the pleasure of traveling. He stopped in Crystal Springs for a quick meal, and he was all the way to Brookhaven before he realized that he wasn't going to travel south after all.

"Can you believe I'm doing this, Sandy?" he asked his moppet dog as he turned the pink bus around and headed north toward Jackson.

Sandy would have growled if she had known that they were going back to see Jessie Wentworth, for she was exceedingly jealous of anybody who came between her and her beloved master. Instead she thumped her tail and licked his ankle.

Blake continued talking to his little dog. "It must be that bit of vulnerability I noticed when George frightened her. I've never felt protective like that toward a woman. What do you suppose has gotten into me?"

Sandy gave his ankle another swipe with her sandpapery tongue. The sound of his voice made her perfectly happy. If she had understood his conversation, she would have taken a bite out of his leg.

"Of course, I can do a magic show in Jackson as well as anywhere," he continued to rationalize aloud. "As a matter of fact, Mrs. Jones wanted me to do a show at Wentworth. Jackson is as good a place as any for my research."

Having come to all those conclusions, Blake resumed his whistling as the 1953 Chevrolet school bus wheezed its way north.

Jessie was late getting home. She had stayed at the store to catch up on work she had missed that morning. Her sedate driving reflected her sagging spirits as she wound slowly up the lane toward Wentworth Manor. The house would be lonely with her parents in Sweden. Face it, she told herself. The house would be lonely without the unusual professor. Even the prospect of seeing her old friend and business associate, Hunter Chadwick, didn't cheer her up.

As she rounded the last curve in the drive, she saw all the cars. There were Mazdas and Hondas and Buicks. There were station wagons and pickup trucks and sports cars. And there, in the midst of it all, was The Joy Bus.

Jessie pulled her car to a teeth-jarring halt. A smile as big as Texas lit her face as she bounded up the steps and hurried across the flagstone veranda. She flung her coat carelessly toward the coat rack and missed. Leaving it spread across the polished floor, she followed the sounds of laughter. They were coming from the direction of her ballroom.

The heavy, carved doors swung open at her touch, and there was Dr. Blake Montgomery, dressed in a tuxedo and magician's cape, pulling brightly colored scarves from the delighted Mrs. Jones's ears. The ballroom was filled with laughing children and equally happy mothers, but Jessie had eyes only for Blake. Seeing him dressed like that, performing his magic tricks, made her believe in childhood dreams and wishing on a star and happily ever after. For a moment she was young and innocent and joyful.

She quietly closed the doors and moved to a chair in the back of the room. Blake saw her and doffed his top hat. Six doves flew out and made a heart-shaped formation in the air. Jessie was enchanted. Her applause was the loudest in the room.

She sat mesmerized through the rest of the show. It seemed that Blake performed every trick specifically for her. Or was that only a part of the illusion? she wondered. Was this man's magic so strong that it blinded her to the truth?

The show ended too soon. Jessie was amazed to find herself groaning with disappointment along with the children. She worked her way to the front, stopping briefly to chat with the people. Most of them were neighbors or friends of Mrs.

Jones, but some of them were strangers to her. It seemed that everybody loved a magic show.

By the time she reached Blake, most of the crowd had thinned out and Mrs. Jones was ushering the rest toward the door.

"What a surprise," she said to Blake. "I didn't expect to be greeted by a magic show."

"I didn't expect to be performing one, either."

He reached up and pulled a yellow rose from behind her ear. She stood very still as he tucked it into her silky black hair.

"Is that why you're here?" she asked. "To perform a show?"

"No. I came back to see you."

"Why?"

"Studying people is a part of my profession, and I find you fascinating."

"You don't pull any punches, do you?"

"No."

"I like that. Most people walk on eggshells around me, saying what they think I want to hear. I get so tired of people seeking my approval."

"I don't need your approval."

"Good." She reached up and touched the rose. "You can stay in the east wing tonight. Dinner is at eight."

He smiled. "You don't pull any punches either, do you?"

"No. I'm glad you came back. There are some things I want to find out about you."

"Can you find out all you need to know in one evening?"

"I don't know about that, Professor. I might have to hold you prisoner at Wentworth Manor."

"I might beg you to let me stay. That blueberry jam cake I had this morning is a powerful incentive."

She laughed. "Then I shall order the cook to make a dozen blueberry jam cakes." She took his arm and led him from the ballroom. "Ordinarily, I would let Mrs. Jones show you to your room, but I want to talk to you. I simply have to know about your bus. Is it standard issue for psychology professors?"

He smiled, partly because of what she had asked but mainly because her hand was tucked into his arm. He liked to have her walking beside him, touching him. "Don't let my colleagues hear you say that. No, that bus and I got together out of plain good luck. I was looking for a vehicle large enough to accommodate my magic act and cheap enough to afford when I read about this one in an auction notice. I was the only bidder. It seemed that nobody else wanted a pink bus."

"It was already painted pink?"

"Yes. I've often speculated about the original owner. He must have been someone with quite a streak of fantasy."

"How do you know the owner was a man? Maybe it was a woman."

"Maybe so. A ballet dancer." He smiled down at her. "Or a department store owner."

She was so caught up in the spell of his smile that she didn't answer right away. When she finally opened her mouth to speak, the front door burst open and in came Hunter Chadwick. His black hair, which defied taming, was bristling around his head, and his black eyes were sparkling as he strode forward to scoop Jessie into his arms.

"Jessie! I see you're still the most beautiful woman in the world."

She squealed with delight and fairly danced him

around the entry hall. "Hunter! How's my favorite toy maker?"

"Confused. Where in the world did you get that god-awful pink bus?"

"It belongs to me," Blake said.

Jessie pulled Hunter forward and made the introductions.

"Dr. Blake Montgomery, this is Hunter Chadwick, dear old friend—"

"Not that old," Hunter interrupted, "but very dear. As a matter of fact, I tried to marry her once but she turned me down flat."

She laughed. "Hush up." She turned to Blake. "Don't pay any attention to a word he says. We were six years old when he proposed. Toy makers are all crazy."

"You're the Chadwick of Chadwick Toys?" Blake asked.

"One and the same. Dolls are my specialty." He pinched Jessie's cheek. "Especially live ones."

That remark coming from anyone else would have ruffled Jessie's feathers. With Hunter, she simply smiled indulgently.

"You just have time to dress before dinner," she said. "I was taking Blake to the east wing, but since this is practically your second home, I'll let you show him the way."

"My pleasure," Hunter said. "This way." With easy charm, he led Blake to the staircase and began to chat.

Jessie heard enough of their conversation to know that Hunter was still an incorrigible womanizer, or so he wanted everybody to think.

"You're a doctor of . . ." Hunter said.

"Psychology. University of Mississippi."

"Aah! The ivied halls of southern pulchritude. Quite a playground you've got there, doctor."

"That sort of thing only happens in the movies."

"Pity."

Jessie stood at the foot of the stairs until they had disappeared, then she went to her suite. She filled a sunken tub with steaming water and bubble bath, piled her hair on top of her head, and hopped in for a long soak. As she slathered herself with jasmine-scented soap, she sang a song from her childhood, "Winnie the Pooh."

Her mother always called it her happy song. Jessie stopped singing long enough to scoop up a handful of bubbles and blow them into the air. She hadn't sung that song in years, but she didn't have to wonder what prompted it now. She knew it was the magic show. That show had made her think of picnics under the oaks with her mother and pony rides in the back pasture with her dad. It had made her think of birthday parties with balloons and days in the park with her friends. It had brought her wonderful forgotten childhood out of hiding.

She rose from the bubbles and wrapped herself in a towel. "Strange," she said aloud. "I wonder why he calls it The Joy Bus?"

She brushed her hair until it was shining. It hung down her back like a bolt of silk. The green velvet dress she put on was simply cut but stunning. It was deeply slashed, front and back, and cinched at the waist by a belt with a diamond buckle.

Jessie reached for her diamond earrings, but her gaze fell on the yellow rose Blake had produced from thin air. She picked it up and tucked it into her hair. It was the only ornament she wore to dinner.

Hunter and Blake, equally resplendent in their tuxedos, were waiting in the sitting room to escort her to dinner. The first thing Blake noticed about Jessie was the rose. He was inordinately pleased.

"I see you wore my flower," he said.

"How could I not? It's the first magic flower I've ever had."

"Then I think you should have more." With a flick of his wrist he produced a bouquet of yellow roses.

"They're gorgeous!" Jessie said. She took the bouquet and placed it in a crystal vase.

"If I could learn that trick," Hunter said, "I'd have every woman in Texas pawing at my front door."

Jessie laughed. "You do anyway, Hunter. They all know what a great guy you are."

"It was no trick," Blake said. "It was magic."

Jessie almost believed him. "Merely illusion," she said as the three of them walked into the dining room.

"Are you sure about that?" Blake asked after they were seated. He tapped his empty coffee cup with a spoon, and a butterfly rose into the air.

Hunter lifted his arms and inspected his coat sleeves. "Why doesn't my tuxedo come equipped with butterflies?"

One kind of magic ended with the arrival of the soup and another kind began. Blake smiled across the soup at Jessie. It was a rare smile that wrapped around her like a rainbow. It was the kind of smile that conveyed reassurance and approval and appreciation. She smiled back, thinking the candlelight must be playing tricks on her, for surely a mere smile couldn't do all those things.

She lifted her soup spoon, determined not to make more of a smile than she ought.

Blake continued to gaze at her across the table,

deep into her eyes. "Delicious," he said. Just that one word. Delicious.

Jessie felt her spine tingle. A primitive instinct told her that he wasn't talking about the soup. She moistened her lower lip with her tongue. If those crystal gray eyes continued to stare at her in that way, as if they were probing right past her velvet gown and viewing her naked flesh, she thought she might faint.

"I'm glad you like it," she said, and she wasn't talking about the soup, either. The signals that passed between them were hot enough to singe the petals of her yellow rose.

Hunter watched them with lively interest. He'd have to be a fool not to know what was going on, and Hunter Chadwick was nobody's fool. He realized that the entire meal would be eaten in silence if he didn't do something. And if he was anything, he was a man of action.

Smiling benignly, Hunter launched into a monologue about the Chadwicks and the Wentworths, who had been friends since Hunter and Jessie were babies.

Although Blake was still watching Jessie as if he wanted to be tasting her rather than the soup, he apparently heard Hunter because he occasionally said, "Hmm."

After the butler had removed the soup dishes and brought the salad, Hunter launched into another monologue about the business relationship between the families. He told Blake that Wentworths department stores had always been one of the biggest markets for Chadwick toys.

"We have dolls that do everything," Hunter explained. "Drink, wet, cry, sing, talk, even skate."

Blake forced his attention away from the delectable Jessie. "They leave nothing to the imagination, do they?" he remarked.

"No. There's always a market for a gimmick," Hunter said. "However, our biggest seller is the baby doll that does nothing at all."

"I'm glad to hear that," Blake said. "It confirms my belief that people enjoy the simple pleasures of life most." As if to prove his theory, he indulged in the simple pleasure of admiring his beautiful hostess.

"It confirms my faith in our advertising department," Hunter said.

If Jessie had been the blushing kind, she would have turned pink under Blake's bold scrutiny. The entire meal was somewhat magical, she decided. If she wasn't careful, she'd be so caught up in the spell that she would forget who she was. A Wentworth. Isolated by her wealth. She forced herself to push the disturbing effect her guest had on her to the back of her mind and enter the conversation.

"Blake, I want to hear more about your belief that people enjoy simple pleasures," she said. "My sales figures seem to refute that. For a people who enjoy simple pleasures, Americans certainly do spend a lot on gadgets."

Blake sensed the change in her. He was sorry to see the magic end. "That's true," he said. "I didn't say we pursue simple pleasures; I said we enjoy them most. Americans have gotten away from the basics and it shows in our attitudes. While I'm on sabbatical, I'm doing research for a book. I'm trying to discover why we have become a melancholy people. We chase frantically around, buying all the latest gadgets and flying to all the best vacation spots in an effort to make ourselves happy. And we're failing miserably."

"Not all of us," Hunter said. "Everything about life makes me happy."

"You're an exception," Jessie said. "You were born happy."

"I'll drink to that," Hunter said.

"Hunter is not really the exception," Blake said. "He's a toy maker; his business is fulfilling childhood dreams. Every day his work immerses him in the innocent world of childhood."

"Let's all drink a toast to childhood dreams," Hunter said. The three of them clicked glasses. "Dream on little ones, and then send your mamas to Wentworths to buy a Chadwick doll."

"Here, here," Jessie said. "Hunter, I want to see your new doll after dinner, but first I want to find out about Blake's bus." She turned to him. Looking into his eyes almost undid her, but she took a deep breath and plunged ahead. "You never did tell me why it's called The Joy Bus. Was it already named when you bought it?"

"No. I thought it was a fitting name for a vehicle that would be involved in my project. It's my belief that Americans have lost their joy because they have lost their innocence."

"An intriguing premise," she said.

"It takes a childlike innocence to believe in magic," he went on. "I do the shows in order to bring people back to that innocence, and in the process I test my theory of the correlation between joy and innocence."

"I'd have to see the proof before I believe that theory," Jessie said.

"Then join me. There's plenty of room in the bus. And I don't bite." He smiled.

At that moment, she'd never wanted anything as much in her life. *Join me.* The words echoed in her mind. She pictured herself on The Joy

Bus, discovering what lay behind his gray eyes, unraveling the mystery of his rare smile. Her palms went damp. Nothing could save her now except her years of experience of being a cool, calm businesswoman.

"Are you serious?" she asked.

"Absolutely."

"Go with him, Jessie," Hunter said. "You haven't taken a real vacation since you started running the stores."

"Are you both crazy?" she asked, but the idea was so appealing she had to bite her tongue to keep from saying yes. There was a certain fairy-tale quality to the idea of traveling in a pink bus with a magician. It was the stuff dreams are made of. She shook her head to clear it of the crazy notions and decided she must be losing her mind even to be considering going off with a virtual stranger.

"I'm crazy," Hunter said, "certifiable."

Blake laughed. "Speak for yourself." He looked at the beautiful woman with his rose tucked into her hair. He had never dreamed of the possibility that she would accompany him. But now that the idea had taken shape, he discovered that he hadn't wanted anything this much in years. He set about trying to convince her.

"I'm sure you have people capable of handling the business in your absence," he said. "Come with me. We'll go south. You'll meet all kinds of people, and you'll get a chance to see my theory proven firsthand."

"How do you know that your return to innocence through magic restores joy?" Her question was skeptical as she skirted the issue of going and concentrated on his philosophy.

"I get feedback. People come to me and tell me

how they feel. Sometimes, if I'm in one place long enough, I get letters."

"You have more faith in the goodness of human nature than I do," she said. "I'll bet you won't find five people in the next three weeks who appreciate your efforts."

Hunter had been following the conversation with lively interest. Now he spoke up. "Take her bet, Blake. Jessie loves a wager."

Blake smiled. "You've on. Only five people."

"Agreed," she said.

"Make it more interesting," Hunter said. "There has to be a winner. What is the wager going to be?"

Jessie smiled at her old friend. She knew that he loved games. Maybe that was why he was perfectly suited to be a maker of toys.

"I hadn't thought of a wager," she said.

"I have," Blake said. "You and I have certain philosophical differences that probably stem from out different life-styles. If I lose, I'll wager one week of walking in your shoes. I'll come to Wentworth Enterprises and be a part of your everyday life in order to gain a better understanding of your philosophy. If you lose, you must spend a week at the university walking in my shoes."

Jessie was stunned speechless by the wager, but Hunter was not.

"That's a wonderful idea, Jessie," he said. "When you and Blake return—"

She interrupted him. "Now wait a minute. I simply made the bet that Blake wouldn't find five grateful people. I never agreed to go with him. And I certainly can't agree to the terms of that wager. The whole proposition is impossible."

"Why?" Blake asked.

"Because I have stores to run. I have responsibilities." To herself she added, because the man who was magic was making her question her philosophy, her way of life. She wanted the enchantment of going, and yet she was afraid to venture beyond the boundaries set by her position and her wealth.

"You have a dozen people who can take care of the business," Hunter said. "Aren't you the one who is always telling me how lonely you get in this big house?"

"Whose side are you on, Hunter?" Jessie asked. He was right about the loneliness. Sometimes, even when her parents were here, she felt as if the huge house were a desert island.

Hunter chuckled. "I didn't know there were sides to this issue. I like Blake and I love you. This idea sounds like fun. What do you have to lose?"

Jessie turned from Hunter to see Blake watching her. His gaze was unsettling. He seemed to be probing beyond her words to her feelings. He seemed to recognize the ambiguities, to sense the struggle. Hunter's question hung in the air as their gazes locked and held.

Blake's mouth curved into a smile. The smile, too, was unsettling. It was gentle, yet knowing.

"What do you have to lose, Jessie?" he asked, echoing Hunter.

Nothing, she thought. Everything. To break the spell of his eyes and his smile, she reached for her drink. The wine sparkled in the light of the chandelier as she lifted the glass.

"I never make deals with strangers," she said.

Three

Jessie couldn't sleep. Magic professors and strange deals and yellow roses kept getting in the way. She tossed the covers aside and got out of bed. Barefoot, she roamed her bedroom, going from window to window, gazing out upon the winter-bleak landscape made even more stark by a pale white moon. As she paced, she felt like a prisoner who wonders what life is like on the outside.

She stopped and pressed her face to a window-pane. There it was, just below her. Blake's ridiculous pink bus. Her smile was sad as she looked at the bus. He she missed a wonderful opportunity or had she been wise? she wondered. Did the bus represent a ticket to freedom, an escape from the restrictions of being a Wentworth; or did it represent a threat, a false promise that would lead to heartbreak? She would never know, for tomorrow Blake would be leaving.

She balled her hand into a fist and struck the windowsill. She didn't want Blake to leave. It was that simple.

Whirling from the window, Jessie stripped off her gown. She tossed it on the bed and pulled black wool slacks and a black turtleneck sweater from her closet. Whatever her reasons—and she wasn't about to stop and consider them—she wanted to keep Blake at Wentworth, at least for a few days. And she knew just how to do it. This time she wouldn't hesitate to rearrange fate.

She chuckled as she dressed. What would he think if she marched into his bedroom and commanded him to stay? He would probably think she was being imperious and high-handed, a wealthy spoiled brat. That was the way she would like to do it, for she was accustomed to giving orders, accustomed to making decisions and following them up with the most direct approach. But not this time. Blake didn't look like the kind of man who could be ordered around. This time she would be subtle. And devious. Even downright underhanded.

Still laughing, she pulled on fur-lined boots and a hooded parka and headed downstairs.

Blake couldn't sleep. He kept thinking of exotic green eyes and midnight hair and a smile that turned his heart upside down. He shoved the covers aside, got out of bed, and walked to the window. The grounds of the Wentworth estate sprawled below him—the curving line of ancient trees, formal gardens crisscrossed by flagstone walkways, a gazebo and fish pond—impressive even in its winter barrenness. His decrepit bus looked out of place in all that splendor, like a garish intruder that had blundered into another world.

He decided he must have been out of his mind to think that Jessie would hop aboard The Joy

Bus and take off to parts unknown with him. He was not normally an impulsive man. Whatever had possessed him to make such an abrupt offer? Certainly not love at first sight. That happened only in books and movies.

Calmly, he explored his motives. The study of the mind had always fascinated him, and he never hesitated to plunder the depths of his own mind, turning the brilliant light of analysis onto those dark corners that produced unexpected behavior.

He didn't know Jessie well enough to conclude that his wanting her to accompany him had stemmed from admiration and respect. He knew that she ran all of the Wentworths department stores, and ran them well. Certainly, he respected that. He admired her beauty. But the measure of a person couldn't be calculated by appearances. No, he thought, it wasn't the things he knew about Jessie that fascinated him. It was the things he didn't know about her. Why had she sparkled at the magic show? Mrs. Jones had said she kept men at arm's length, yet she was so warm with Hunter. What would it take to bring that warmth out of hiding? And that smile! Only people with a deep reservoir of joy could smile like that. He could sit for hours just contemplating Jessie's smile.

He had to know her better. That's all there was to it. Even if he couldn't convince her to go with him on The Joy Bus, he had to spend some time with her. A few days at least.

Turning from the window, Blake sat in a chair to think. How could he arrange a lengthy visit? There was no good reason to stay longer, and Jessie had not invited him to extend the visit. Why should she? Exchanged looks across a dining table weren't reason enough. Or were they?

He rose abruptly and began to dress. Dr. Blake Montgomery knew that he *had* to be with Jessie a few more days. And he was going to make certain it happened. He was going to do something he had never done before—be devious.

He was smiling when he went out the door and down the stairs.

Jessie knew of one sure-fire way to keep Blake on the Wentworth estate—disable his bus. Fortunately, she didn't have to know a thing about mechanics to accomplish this feat. She knew from hard-earned experience that cars won't go when the lights are left on.

She laughed aloud as she stepped outside and headed toward the bus. Her cheeks and the tip of her nose immediately tingled from the frigid night air. She snuggled the hood closer around her face, wishing she had remembered to wear gloves. It was so cold that even the stars seemed to be frozen in the India ink sky.

She hurried to the bus and pushed against the front door. She had been right in thinking Blake was a trusting man. The door was unlocked. Quickly she climbed the steps. The interior of the bus was only slightly warmer than it was outside.

Slapping her hands together for warmth, Jessie knelt beside the dashboard. In the dim moonlight she searched the panel for the light switch. There it was, on the other side of the steering column. Her breath fogged the windows as she reached for it.

Suddenly she froze. What was that noise? She sat still, listening, scarcely breathing. There it was again. Footsteps. Her heart pounded against her rib cage. Could it be a burglar? How could they get past her security guards? She ducked her head lower so she wouldn't be visible through the bus window.

The footsteps seemed to be coming closer. They stopped for a moment, then a new sound rent the air. A metallic squeaking and banging made the hairs on Jessie's arms stand on end. The hood of the bus suddenly loomed into her vision. Good lord. Somebody was trying to steal the bus.

She squeezed her cold hands together and tried not to panic. A dozen crazy thoughts darted through her mind. Was she getting the well-known just desserts for her interference with fate? Would she be carried off in the bus and held for ransom? Not if she could help it.

She crept toward the back of the bus, determined to sneak out and alert her security guards. She blundered into Blake's magic props and held her breath as they banged against the side of the bus. Would the burglar hear? She squeezed her cold hands together, waiting. The only sound she heard was a muffled clanking that seemed to be coming from under the hood.

Creeping on all fours, she continued her way toward the back of the bus. A curtain brushed against her face, and she stifled a scream. She placed a hand over her banging heart, pushed the curtain aside, and crept past a cot. By the time she reached the back door, she had thoroughly repented of her wicked ways and decided she would never again mess with fate.

She reached for the door handle. It was icy cold. She pushed against the door, but it refused to budge. Biting her lower lip, she tried again. The back door swung open, and Jessie jumped out of The Joy Bus.

She didn't waste any time in trying to locate the

burglar. She knew that he was around the corner of the bus, only a heartbeat away. Her long legs fairly flew across the frozen grass as she sprinted toward the security guards' station.

Suddenly her feet were jerked out from under her and she was on the ground. She thrashed about, trying to scream, but the man who had tackled her was astraddle her hips and had one hand over her mouth. Her hair fanned out on the moonlit grass as her parka hood fell aside.

"Good Lord," Blake Montgomery said. "I thought you were a burglar." He jumped off her and helped her up.

"I thought the same thing about you." She shivered.

He pulled her hood around her face, tucking her dark hair inside. "Are you all right? Did I hurt you?" His hands lingered on her cheeks as he prolonged the task of fixing her hair.

"Only my feelings. I thought I could outrun anybody. I used to be pretty good at the hundred-yard dash."

"You've never been up against a cross-country runner before." He chafed her cold hands between his gloved ones. "Let's go inside before you freeze."

"I think I already have. My nose feels like an icicle."

He took both of her hands in his right hand and rubbed her nose with his left. "What are you doing out here?" he asked as they walked toward the house.

"Turning on the lights so the bus won't go. What are you doing?"

"Disconnecting the battery cables."

They both roared with laughter.

"If you had wanted to stay longer," she said, "why didn't you just ask?"

"Maybe I was afraid of being turned down. If you had wanted me to stay longer, why didn't you just extend an invitation?"

"I don't know. Maybe it was because I didn't want to appear domineering."

"Are you?"

"Sometimes."

"I like an honest woman." He stopped walking and looked down at her. "You know I'm going to try to convince you to go with me."

Maybe that was why she wanted him to stay, she thought. Maybe she wanted to be convinced. She looked away from his disturbing gaze and resumed the walk to the house. Going off on The Joy Bus would be crazy; but then everything had been crazy since Blake Montgomery came. Who would have dreamed that she would be sashaying around at midnight trying to sabotage a pink bus? She'd better regain her perspective or there was no telling what she would do next.

"I can't go," she said.

"Why not?"

"I've already told you."

"Tell me again," he said. "I think your first answer was a smoke screen."

He pushed open the front door, and they entered the warm hallway.

Her parka hood fell backward as she tipped her head up and looked at him. The midnight silk hair framed her rosy cheeks. "It was a smoke screen."

Blake caught his breath at her beauty. She was so stunning that he forgot what they had been talking about. For a small eternity he stood in the hallway, his eyes devouring her face.

"You're beautiful," he said.

She remained still under his scrutiny. Never

before had a man's gaze made her feel this way, she thought, warm and glowing inside, as if sunshine had been poured through her veins.

"I'm cold," she whispered.

He took a step toward her. "Is that an invitation?"

"Yes, but only a small one. Just for a warm-me-up hug."

He scooped her into his arms and hugged her close while she was still talking. Her voice was muffled against his chest. "You're a stranger. For all I know you could be a con artist. Somebody after my money." She snuggled closer as his hands slipped under her parka and rubbed her back, warming it with a wonderful friction that would have been erotic if she had let herself think about it. "The Joy Bus looks innocent enough," she continued, "and heaven knows the magic is harmless. But how do I know it's not an elaborate trick?"

"You have my word of honor."

"How do I know you're a man of your word? I'm accustomed to security checks and complex contracts drawn up by a team of high-priced lawyers."

Blake took his hands from under her parka and put them on her shoulders. Gently, he pushed her back. "Only a man of honor could let you go with a small warm-me-up hug." He smiled down at her.

It was the same bewitching smile she had seen at dinner. The sunshine in her veins turned to fire. "And what would a not-so-honorable man do?"

Their gazes locked, and their breathing sounded harsh in the tense stillness of the hallway. Jessie bit her lower lip, waiting for his answer. Even the Wentworth ancestors seemed to be bending down from their portraits to see what the magic professor would say.

His smile looked as if it had never been seen except by the woman standing beside him. "Someday I'll show you," he said.

Jessie almost believed him. She almost believed she could climb aboard The Joy Bus and ride off into the sunset with the man who was magic. She almost believed she could forget that her money made her an easy target, that she could allow warm-me-up hugs to turn into passion without fear of being used. She almost believed there could be a common ground between his world and hers.

She smiled. "You truly are a master of illusion. I almost believe you."

"Since I'll be staying at Wentworth for a few days . . ." He paused, giving her time to dispute him. When she didn't, he continued, ". . . I'll have plenty of time to perform another feat of magic."

"What's that?"

"Banishing your skepticism."

"Good night, Blake."

"Good night, Jessie."

After Jessie and Blake had vacated the hall, two other people tiptoed through the front door, first one and then the other.

Mrs. Jones turned from the coat rack as Hunter came in. "Matchmaking again?" she asked.

Hunter unwrapped the wool scarf around his neck and laughed. "You caught me red-handed. I went out to disconnect the hot wire that runs to the coil on The Joy Bus."

Mrs. Jones held out her hands. She was holding the spark plugs.

After they had stopped laughing, Hunter said, "I had a quick security check run on the professor before dinner—to protect Jessie. He's everything he said he was. He's a hundred percent okay."

"Poppycock. I could have told you that. All a body had to do is look into the man's face and read it." Mrs. Jones dropped the spark plugs into her pocket. "Hunter, someday you're going to meet a woman who makes you forget about security checks."

Hunter pinched her cheeks. "You and Jessie have already turned me down. I'm not holding my breath."

Blake was fascinated. He had come to work with Jessie and was sitting at the back of the conference room while she conducted a meeting. There was no doubt about it, he thought. Jessie was completely in charge. The department managers sought her opinion and generally bowed to her judgment. Even the accountants respected her advice.

He noticed that she was as much at home with a financial statement as she was with a purchase order. She was respected not simply because of her name but because of her knowledge. She had earned their respect.

He was glad to see that. Too often incompetents were put in positions of authority because of who they were rather than what they knew. That was definitely not true in the case of Jessie.

She brought the meeting to a close, and he watched her department managers and accountants and attorneys file past her, stopping for a polite word, a murmured thanks. She smiled at them, accepting their praise. Her smile was sincere; the praise was genuine; but Blake noticed the distance between her and her employees. Nobody called her Jessie; nobody touched her; nobody stopped for a friendly chat. It was almost as if she were on a pedestal, as if her name had automatically set her apart.

She was surrounded by people, and yet she was isolated. It was the same isolation Blake felt in the classroom, in the midst of people who strictly observed the limits of a teacher–student relationship. The major difference between him and Jessie was that he had the camaraderie of his colleagues. Except for Hunter, she seemed to have no one.

"Are we boring you?" Jessie had crossed the conference room and was standing beside his chair.

He stood up. "On the contrary. I'm always fascinated by people who do their jobs well."

She seemed pleased by the compliment, and laughed. "I thought you might be getting restless. You've suffered through so many meetings this morning."

"Three, to be exact. Not suffered, though. Enjoyed."

"You're a very patient man. I'm surprised you didn't stay at Wentworth with Hunter. He would have been much more entertaining than all these meetings."

"I didn't go out in the dead of winter and disconnect battery cables so I could be with Hunter."

She didn't know why the remark flustered her. The bright executive who was perfectly at ease conducting meetings nervously squeezed her briefcase handle. "Don't tell him that. Hunter is a people collector. He thinks everybody is as eager for his company as he is for theirs."

Blake reached out and took her free hand. "I don't want to talk about Hunter."

Jessie thought his hand felt wonderful on hers.

She wondered how that hand would feel on her face, on her body. The board room was empty except for the two of them. For an insane moment she thought of winding herself around him just to see how it would feel.

She moistened her dry lips with her tongue. "What do you want to talk about?" Her voice was barely a whisper.

Without speaking, Blake loosed her hold on the briefcase. His thumbs pressed small, erotic circles in her palms.

The room became so warm that Jessie thought she might have to douse her head in cold water if she ever got out of there in one piece. Blake's eyes seemed to be lit from within by the sun. They gazed intently at her, increasing the temperature by a good fifteen degrees.

"I want to talk about you," he said.

His gaze never left her face. She was caught by his gray eyes, was drowning in them. Never had a man looked at her in that way. She decided that nothing would be more wonderful than just spending the afternoon basking in that look. It was penetrating, intense. The look in his eyes was pure sex.

Their breathing became harsh in the closed room. If they had been two other people, they might have come together in a passionate embrace. But they were Jessie Wentworth and Dr. Blake Montgomery. They were held apart by honorable intentions and leftover fears. They were separated by philosophies and life-styles.

Blake was the first to break the spell. He released her hands. "This morning you mentioned a tour of your store."

"So I did," she said with more intent than briskness. "Let's take that tour, then we'll go back home. I've taken the afternoon off."

"You didn't have to do that for me. I'm perfectly content here at the store."

She smiled. "Do you think I went out in the dead of winter to turn on your lights just so I could be at the store?"

He laughed. "Like I said, I love an honest woman."

Jessie whisked him through the store and back to Wentworth Manor. And always, the look was between them. She had never been so eager to leave her work behind.

She bounded through the front door, tossed her sable coat toward the rack, missed, and left it there for the maid to pick up. Without comment, Blake hung the coat up.

"Do you like horses?" Jessie asked.

"I like all animals."

Hearing her master's voice, Sandy bounded around the corner and leaped into his arms.

Jessie laughed. "I forgot about your menagerie." She reached out to pet Sandy's head and was rewarded with a snarl. "Good Lord, that dog hates me."

"She's not quick to make friends, but she'll come around." He opened his arms and let Sandy jump to the floor. "What were you saying about horses?"

"We'll go riding. The stable's out back. Better wear plenty of clothes."

Hunter appeared from the direction of the library holding a brandy in one hand and a book in the other. "Did you mention riding?"

"Yes," Jessie said. "Do you want to come?"

"A pastime of the idle rich, my dear." He winked at her. "I have more important things to do. I'm planning a party."

Jessie groaned. "Not again, Hunter. Every time you come you plan one of those gosh-awful parties."

"The trouble with you, Jessie," Hunter said, "is that you don't have enough fun in your life."

"The Joy Bus could remedy that," Blake said.

Jessie dismissed them with a wave of her hand. "What is this, a conspiracy? I'll see you at the stable in twenty minutes, Blake." She ran lightly up the stairs.

In her bedroom Jessie whirled around singing her Pooh Bear song. It was amazing what a difference people in the house made, she thought. Of course, Hunter always livened things up, but Blake seemed to fill empty spaces that she hadn't even known were there. Sitting across the table from her, he had been a magical presence, a man who lent sparkle and joy to the meal. And standing in the hallway last night, he had been solid and reassuring. Except for Hunter, there wasn't another man in her life that she would ask to give her a warm-me-up hug. What was there about Blake that had prompted that request? Maybe it was the look in his eyes. She didn't know. All she knew was that the relationship felt good.

By the time she had finished dressing, her room looked as if it had been caught up in a tornado and whirled all the way to Kansas and back. Rejected clothes were strewn across the bed, the floor, and the chairs. Jessie had finally settled on a blue wool tweed riding habit. Flinging a leather jacket across her shoulder, she headed toward the stable—and Dr. Blake Montgomery.

Four

Blake was waiting for Jessie inside the stable.

"I see you've made friends with Whirlwind," she said.

He rubbed the velvety nose of the Appaloosa. "I hope that name isn't significant."

Smiling, he watched her cross the stable. Pale fingers of winter sun, filtering down from the loft window, caressed her face and gilded her hair. She was so breathtakingly beautiful that she seemed unreal. He had to pinch himself to be sure she wasn't a vision.

"I thought you said you could ride," she said, laughing.

"I can, but I've always ridden horses with names like Poke Along and Glue Factory."

"Then you're in for a treat."

She stopped less than an arm's length away from him and reached out to pat the horse's nose. Their hands made brief contact. The electricity of that touch seared along Blake's nerve endings. The urge to pull her into his arms and kiss her was so strong that he had to shove his hands into his pockets to keep from giving in. He wondered if he would be able ride without making a complete fool of himself. He had always considered himself to be a self-possessed, sensible man. The primitive force of the sexual urges Jessie incited in him startled him. He decided he would have to reassess his ideas about relationships. He had always believed they were like houses, laid on a solid foundation and built slowly, brick by brick. What was happening to him now seemed more like a lightning bolt or a flash flood, a sudden, capricious act of nature.

His gaze sought and held hers. "Just being with you is a treat, Jessie."

Jessie was once more under the spell of his look. As his eyes probed deep into hers she considered chucking the afternoon ride and taking him up into the hayloft. She thought about plunging into a full-blown relationship and forgetting the consequences. She longed for everything that look seemed to offer.

There was no sound in the quiet stable except their own harsh breathing and the soft snorts of the horses. Jessie and Blake faced each other, caught in the spell of the passion that arced between them.

"Which horses do you want me to saddle, Miss Wentworth?" the groom asked from the door of the tack room. The sound of his voice broke the spell.

Jessie reluctantly dragged her gaze away from Blake. "Whirlwind and Satin Doll." She nodded toward the Appaloosa and a palomino. "And Carl," she added as he turned back to the tack room to get the saddles, "we won't need you later. Blake and I will unsaddle the horses."

Carl gave her a quizzical look. Miss Wentworth rarely unsaddled her own horse. Not that she considered herself too highfalutin for such work, he mused. She was just always too busy with important things like running her daddy's stores. Her stores now, he corrected himself.

"Very well, Miss Wentworth," he said. There was just no accounting for the ways of the rich, he decided as he saddled the two horses.

Jessie swung easily into Satin Doll's saddle. "I'm letting you ride Whirlwind, Blake." She laughed as he mounted. "Don't look so grim. He knows the bridle path better than I do, and he's not nearly as wicked as his name."

The Appaloosa, eager to be outside, plunged through the open double doors. Blake almost came unseated, then recovered and reined the horse to a stop.

"Did somebody forget to tell him?" he asked.

Jessie trotted up to him. "Are you sure this is what you want to do? You can always go back inside. Hunter is probably sitting before the fire sipping brandy."

"A civilized pursuit, but not nearly as exciting as this. Besides, I prefer the present company. I'll get my riding legs in a minute. Lead on, Beautiful Lady."

"You asked for it. Follow me." Jessie leaned forward in the saddle. Satin Doll, catching the exhilaration of her mistress, flared her nostrils and tossed her white mane as she galloped up the bridle path into the woods.

Blake urged Whirlwind forward. He ducked under a low-hanging branch as the Appaloosa thundered after Jessie.

She rode the way she drove, he thought, with

dare-devil ease. He leaned forward in the saddle, trusting the stallion's instincts.

Jessie felt a marvelous sense of freedom, as if nothing in the world existed except the woods and the two people on horses, as if nothing mattered except the moment.

The lake was just ahead of her, its waters a slate blue under the winter sun. Glancing over her shoulder, she yelled at Blake, "Come on, slowpoke. I'll race you to the lake."

"You're on. And I plan to win." He gave the big stallion its head, but even with the extra burst of speed he couldn't catch Jessie. She and the palomino were waiting beside the lake when he got there.

"I thought you said you planned to win," she said brushing back a lock of hair the wind had whipped into her face.

"I did win."

"No, you didn't. I got here first."

"But I won anyway." His smile was enigmatic.

"Explain that, please."

"I never intended to pass you. I was too entranced with the view."

"The woods are lovely, even in the winter."

"I wasn't talking about the trees. I was talking about you."

Color that had nothing to do with the wind suffused her cheeks. She felt as pleased as a schoolgirl.

"The way you fit into a saddle should be declared illegal, Jessie."

"The way you use your charm should be outlawed, Professor. You must have students fighting to get into your classes."

Smiling, he slid from the saddle. "Not so you'd

notice." He reached up and put his arms around her waist.

She laughed. "I can dismount alone, but it's not nearly as much fun as this. Carry on, Professor."

He lifted her easily from the saddle and swung her down beside him. Still holding her, he said, "I think that's the way they used to do it in the movies."

"So do I." She felt breathless as she looked up at him. "Except you left out the best part."

Without thinking she lifted her lips to his. He needed no further invitation. The kiss started as a brief pleasure, an extension of the easy friendship between them. But as his lips moved across hers it grew to unbridled passion. Automatically her arms circled his neck. Her fingers found the sunshine hair at the back of his head.

His tongue plunged into the warm depths of her mouth and she groaned in undisguised pleasure. He hauled her close against his hips. She could feel the muscled strength of his legs, the wide expanse of his chest. She kissed him mindlessly, letting go of all her caution, seizing the moment without regard to the consequences.

"Jessie," he murmured against her lips. "Beautiful Jessie."

"Don't stop." The words were a broken plea against his mouth. "I don't want you to stop."

His arms tightened around her, and he rocked her against his hips. There was no mistaking his desire. All the pent-up passion of the candlelight dinner and the office tour came rushing to the surface. And this time, neither of them tried to deny it.

They clung together until their lips felt bruised. They kissed until the heat of their desire threatened to consume them. A gentle nudge from Satin

Doll brought them out of their passion-drugged state.

Blake and Jessie exchanged surprised looks, as if neither could believe the intensity of their feelings.

"I meant it just to be a small kiss," she said.

"Like the warm-me-up hug last night?"

"Yes."

He pulled her jacket closer around her shoulders, then cupped her face with his hands. "You make me forget, Jessie."

"Forget what?"

"All my theories about relationships."

"You make me forget, Blake. You make me forget about—" She broke off suddenly. There was no use dredging up painful memories, she decided. There was no need to spoil a perfectly lovely ride by talking about betrayal. There was no need to point out the obvious: rich women had to be careful.

He waited for her to continue. He knew that she believed her money was a barrier to relationships. She had already hinted as much. He hoped she would talk about the broken engagement. Sometimes talking about the past helped release its hold.

Still touching her face, he looked deep into her eyes. "Trust me, Jessie."

"I do, but . . ."

"But what?"

"You make me believe things that aren't real. You make me believe I'm free to be ordinary. I keep forgetting that you're a master of illusion."

"And you're the mistress of skepticism. Believe what you feel. Learn to trust your instincts."

"Is that what you do, Blake?"

"Yes. In spite of all my carefully acquired philosophies about life, I've learned to go with my instincts. And right now they're telling me to scoop you into my arms and ride off into the sunset."

"Whose sunset? Yours or mine?"

Her question had the intended effect. He dropped his hands from her face as he recognized the barrier she was erecting between them. "They're the same, Jessie." He gave her a leg up into her saddle. His smile was magic as he looked up at her. "I'll show you if you'll come with me on The Joy Bus."

"Professor, you've already tempted me enough for one day. Right now, all I want to do is get back to the stable before my nose freezes off."

"I know a better way of keeping your nose warm."

"I do, too, but it's too dangerous." She slapped her reins lightly against Satin Doll. "Race you back to the stable," she called over her shoulder.

As he watched her gallop into the woods, he had second thoughts about being honorable. What he wanted to do was rip off her riding habit and take her right there beside the lake.

"Good Lord, Blake Montgomery," he said aloud as he mounted Whirlwind. "You're becoming a savage." He urged the stallion into a gallop. With the wind against his face, he grinned. "It's not such a bad feeling. I guess there's a little beast in every man."

The stallion paid him no attention. He was too busy trying to shorten the distance between himself and the warm stable.

Jessie was already dismounted and unsaddling her mare when Blake returned to the stable.

She grinned up at him. "What took you so long?"

"Some of us old fogies travel at a more sedate pace than you young hellions." He slid off the horse and began to unbuckle the girth. "Besides, you miss all the scenery going at breakneck speed."

"We would never make good traveling companions. I'd be bored stiff poking along in that bus."

Blake's heart lifted at her words. So she was thinking about coming with him, he exulted.

"No, you wouldn't," he said. "The people along the way keep it interesting. When I was in Nashville I picked up a group of teenagers, musicians, who had tried to make it in the entertainment world and failed." He carried their saddles into the tack room.

After he returned, Jessie asked, "You picked up hitchhikers?"

"Not exactly. They were at my magic show. Afterwards they came backstage and we talked. They were disillusioned young people who were simply trying to get back home to Texas."

"How did you know they didn't plan to hit you on the head and steal your bus?"

"Instinct."

"I rely on facts, not feelings."

"If I weren't still being honorable, I'd give your feelings another test, Jessie."

"In the hay, Professor?"

He laughed. "Yes. Another tactic I learned from watching old movies."

She looked from Blake to the fragrant pile of hay in the empty stall beside Satin Doll. At that moment she wanted to take his hand and lead him to the hay. She wanted to forget everything except the magic man beside her. But she couldn't. She was no ordinary woman. She was Jessie Wentworth, the woman in the ivory tower.

"You've been watching the wrong movies," she said. "I'll see if Hunter can dig up one of his for you." Impulsively, she took his hand. "Come on, let's head toward the house before I change my mind about that hay."

"I wish you would."

She gave him a sidelong glance. "If you keep looking so delicious, I will. Let's talk about something safe."

"Hunter?"

She laughed. "Yes. My wonderful, safe friend Hunter."

"What movies does he watch?"

"Bugs Bunny."

"I should have guessed. It's natural that a toy maker would love cartoons."

"He's just a happy kid at heart."

"And perfect proof of my theory."

"The correlation between the return to innocence and joy?"

"That's the one."

"I don't want to talk about that, either. I want to drink hot chocolate with you and warm my nose and forget that we kissed."

"I can handle the first two suggestions, but the third is going to be impossible."

"Give it the old college try, Professor."

"That's easier said than done."

They shed their coats as they entered the warm house.

"How does hot chocolate sound to you?" Jessie asked.

"Delicious."

She reached for the intercom button.

"Wait." He put his hand on hers. "Don't call anybody. Let's make it ourselves."

"Why?"

"It's more fun that way. Besides, I have ulterior motives."

"Getting me alone in the kitchen?"

"No. Seeing if you can cook. The Joy Bus needs a new cook." The way he said it, with laugh lines crinkling at his eyes, she knew he was joking.

"You lose on two counts. Wild horses couldn't force me to cook, and I'm not going on that pink bus." She led the way to the kitchen.

"I'll make you change your mind."

"I have to admit the temptation is great."

He put his hands on her shoulders and spun her around. "Then what's stopping you?"

"I try not to yield to temptation more than once a day. The lake was my day's quota."

He smiled. "I wonder if a little magic would make you change your mind." He leaned down and kissed her. It was a gentle kiss, sweet and brief and giving.

"That's not magic," she said.

"What would you call it?"

"Just a kiss."

"Kisses are magic, particularly if they're done with the right person."

Jessie didn't want to think about that just now. She was afraid that Blake was correct: kisses *were* magic with the right person. But how was she to know when she had the right person?

She stepped back from him. "When somebody invents a foolproof method for determining the right person, let me know." Only her turbulent eyes showed the pain behind her light statement. She spun away from him and began to rummage through the pantry. "Now where do you suppose the cook keeps the chocolate?"

"Right here." Blake reached over her shoulder and took the chocolate from the top shelf.

With him standing so close, Jessie felt that rush of pleasure that always made her want to be in his arms. She tried to squash it, but only succeeded in taming it for the moment.

"I'll take that." She turned the box over and began to read the label. "Now what does it say about making chocolate?"

"I don't need to read the label. Just show me the pans."

"*I'm* making this chocolate."

He laughed. "Aren't you the woman who said wild horses couldn't make you cook?"

"I've changed my mind."

"Why?"

"Do you always have to know the reason for everything, Professor?"

"Yes."

"I'll tell you why. I've never seen anything I wouldn't try at least once. And besides that, as long as I have my mind on cooking I won't be tempted by your talk of magic and instincts and joy." She brandished the chocolate box at him. "I'm *not* going on The Joy Bus. Sit over there, Professor, while I engineer this masterpiece."

Grinning hugely, Blake sat at the kitchen table and watched Jessie try to locate a pan.

"Now where does the cook keep those blasted things?" she muttered. Her search was punctuated by the banging of cabinet doors and the rattling of cooking utensils. "Damned crazy place for a coffee pot." She plopped it onto the countertop. "Who would put a waffle iron there?" It joined the coffeepot. "Would you look at that?" A punch bowl and twelve cups flanked the waffle iron. "Where the devil is a pan?" She slung a box of graham crackers and a bag of flour onto the countertop. The flour sack popped a hole and left a trail of white across the kitchen floor.

"Need any help?" Blake asked.

She pushed her hair back from her face, smearing flour along her cheek. "I'm doing fine by myself."

He chuckled. "I can see that."

"Don't you dare laugh at me, Blake Montgomery."

"I'm not laughing at you, Beautiful Lady. I'm laughing because making chocolate has never been this much fun before."

"You call this fun? I call it slave labor." Suddenly, she smiled. "Aha! There's a pot." She dragged an oversize galvanized aluminum pot from the cabinet and put it on the range. "Now I'm in business."

"Don't you think it's a little large?"

"*I'm* doing the cooking, Professor."

"Carry on. But if you need any help, don't hesitate to ask for it."

"I won't need it. I'm going to have fun, even if it kills me." She picked up the tin of chocolate and read the label again. "Umhmm. Just as I thought." She got the milk and poured half a gallon into the pot. "Whoops! I guess I'll just have to use more chocolate."

She added more chocolate to compensate for the extra milk, then added more sugar to sweeten the extra chocolate. She stirred her concoction vigorously, decided she needed more milk to compensate for her overdose of chocolate, and then declared that she needed another pot. By the time she had finished making two cups of hot chocolate, there were four huge pots bubbling away on the range.

"My masterpiece," she announced. Giving Blake a triumphant smile, she added, "I told you I could make chocolate."

"I never doubted it for a minute." He looked at her lovely face, streaked with flour and dabbed with sugar and chocolate. "It looks good enough to eat."

"Well, help yourself. There's plenty. You can have all you want."

"If I took all I wanted, I'd probably be arrested."

"Are we talking about the same thing?"

"No."

"I thought not." She whirled around and gave the chocolate a vigorous stir. "It has lumps."

"It's perfect."

"You haven't tasted it, yet." She poured chocolate into two china cups and handed one to Blake.

"Yes, I have," he said. "It's perfect."

"If you don't stop that, Professor, I'm going to rue the day I sabotaged your bus."

"All right. I promise to behave." He took the cup and set it on the table. "You're so damned beautiful you turn me upside down." He sipped the chocolate. "You're right; it does have lumps."

"This was your idea of fun, not mine." Jessie sat down beside him and sipped her chocolate. "Lord, this stuff's awful. It needs to be recalled."

"Are you having a party without me?" Hunter asked as he stuck his head through the doorway.

Jessie smiled at him. Hunter never merely walked into a room, she thought. He made an entrance; he filled a room with exuberance and liveliness and a kind of magnetism that was uniquely his.

"Join us," she said. She was glad for the company. Her attraction for Blake was getting out of hand. A simple cup of hot chocolate had turned into a sizzling occasion that made her feel hot and bothered inside.

Hunter peered into the bubbling pots. "You expecting a crowd, Jessie?"

"No. That started out as chocolate for two," she said.

"It looks like chocolate for two hundred. I'd fire that cook if I were you."

"Pour yourself a cup and give us your verdict. I did the cooking."

Hunter chuckled. "You've always said wild horses couldn't drag you into the kitchen. What brought about that miracle, Jessie? As if I didn't know." He poured a cup of chocolate and joined them at the table. "Do you have plenty of life insurance, Blake? Let me tell you about the time she made mud pies. She made me eat every blasted one of them."

Blake laughed. "I'm glad you warned me. We could be here until the middle of next week trying to drink all her chocolate."

Jessie leaned over and patted his cheek. "But think of all the fun you'll have, Professor, just you and the lumpy chocolate."

"And the chocolate-spattered cook." Blake captured her hands and planted a kiss on each palm. Then he pulled a red scarf from her shirt sleeve and carefully wiped the smudges on her cheeks. "A little magic will take care of that."

Hunter didn't miss a thing—the glow on Jessie's face, the leap of passion in Blake's eyes. "I do believe magic beats being filthy rich," he said.

Nobody paid him any mind.

The next few days passed in a blur of pleasure for Blake and Jessie. They rode the estate, shared quiet moments beside the fire, and enjoyed candlelight dinners.

While they were enjoying themselves, Hunter's party grew and grew. It started as a small bash of twenty people and turned into a costume ball for seventy-five, complete with orchestra.

When Blake and Jessie complained that they didn't want to take the time to go out and rent costumes, he cheerfully had the costume shop come to them. A van from Pandora's Costume Shop pulled up before Wentworth Manor and unloaded fifteen boxes of costumes.

"Look at this," Hunter said as he plopped a ten-gallon hat onto his head. It covered his ears and settled onto the bridge of his nose. "What do you think?"

"I don't believe all Texans were meant to be cowboys," Jessie said.

"Aw, shucks, ma'am. I've always wanted to be a cowboy. I was thinking of riding into the ballroom on Whirlwind." Hunter took off the hat and picked up a masked avenger costume.

"You'd do it, too." Turning to Blake, she said, "He's incorrigible."

"So I've noticed," Blake said, but he wasn't really that interested. He had eyes only for Jessie. "What costume are you wearing tonight?"

"This is a masked ball," she said. "Don't you like surprises?"

"Only if you're a part of them. Give me a hint."

She picked up two boxes and started out the door. "Professor, you'll have to use magic to find me tonight." Flashing her brilliant smile, she swept from the room.

"You won't need magic to find her," Hunter said after she had gone. "She always wears a red costume."

Blake laughed. "Not that I would have had any trouble picking her out of a crowd, but thanks, friend."

"Any time. I enjoy playing cupid."

$$• \quad • \quad •$$

Hunter had been right, Blake thought as he looked across the crowded ballroom. Jessie was wearing red. She was stunning in an exotic red sari that bared one shoulder. Her raven's wing hair was swept up in an elegant French twist that left tendrils curling seductively around her neck. A sequined mask partially hid her face.

He lounged against a marble column and studied her. The elegant setting suited her, he thought. She looked like a finely polished ruby in the center of an expensive crown. This was her world, a world of lavish parties and instant gratification. Wave a greenback and orchestras appear. Whip out a checkbook and orchids fill every corner.

He watched her move through the crowd. Although she smiled and chatted with the guests, she still gave the impression of a woman in an ivory tower, isolated and untouchable. He sensed that it was more than her money that set her apart, more than a broken engagement. Wealth didn't necessarily dictate isolation, and broken engagements didn't always mean permanent disillusionment. What had she said beside the lake? *You make me forget that I'm not free to be ordinary.* Why? he wondered. Why didn't she feel free to be ordinary? He was filled with a desire to find out. He wanted to look into her mind and her heart. He wanted to have her beside him, to show her his world, the world of ordinary people. He wanted to release whatever chains bound her. He wanted to be her hero, her rescuer. He wanted to be a true magician.

Shaking his head, he laughed at himself. Hell, he thought, all his motives weren't that noble and grand. He wanted to be her lover. More than a hero, more than a knight in shining armor, more than a magician, he wanted to be an ordinary man loving an ordinary woman. He wanted to memorize her body with his hands. He wanted to kiss her until he released that explosive passion he had felt beside the lake. Then he wanted to take her in a sweet, savage blaze of glory.

"She does that to a man, doesn't she?" Hunter said. Blake hadn't even heard his approach.

"It's a damned good thing this costume has a cape," Blake said.

Hunter laughed. "You're not the first man to feel that way just looking at her." He handed Blake a glass of champagne. "Drink up. It looks like it's going to be a long evening for you."

Blake took the drink. "What's holding her back, Hunter? Why doesn't she feel free to be ordinary?"

"Did she tell you that?"

"Yes."

Hunter was thoughtful as he gazed across the room at Jessie. When she looked in his direction, he lifted his glass in silent salute to her.

"She'll tell you when the time is right for her," he said to Blake. "But I'll tell you this much: In all the years I've known Jessie, I've never seen her as relaxed and easy around a man other than me as she is with you."

Blake put a hand on his shoulder. "Thanks. She's lucky to have a friend like you."

"That works both ways. She's a superfine lady. Go after her."

Blake laughed. "That's exactly my intention."

Hunter watched Blake weave through the crowd toward Jessie. He noted the determined stride, the squared shoulders. Lifting his glass toward them, he said aloud, "You've met your match, Jessie." Then he turned his attention to a shapely southern belle in a bunny costume that wasn't much more than a cottontail and two pink ears. It was brief to the point of indecency.

"Well, hello, darlin'," he drawled. "I was hoping you'd hop into my life."

"Are you talkin' to little ole me?" The bunny wiggled her cottontail.

"Sure 'nuff, honey." He took her arm and escorted her toward the bar. Loneliness, he thought, made strange bedfellows. He glanced over his shoulder long enough to see that Blake and Jessie had found each other. Then his friends were forgotten as he got on with the business of playing Hunter Chadwick, rich Texas playboy.

Jessie couldn't suppress her smile as Blake touched her elbow. In spite of his cavalier costume, she'd had no trouble recognizing him. She'd know that corn silk hair and those wonderful mobile lips anywhere. Not to mention those inviting shoulders.

"Let's find a quiet corner," he said.

"I don't go off with strange men."

"Then let me introduce myself." He bent down and took her mouth swiftly. Nothing touched except their lips, but even so, it was a kiss that could have set fire to the ballroom.

When it was over, she put her hand on his chest and pushed him back an inch. "You mustn't keep doing that, Blake."

"Why? Don't you enjoy it?"

"The trouble is, I enjoy it too much."

"I don't consider that a problem: I consider it a personal triumph." He smiled. "Do you think dancing would be safe for us?"

"Probably not, but we can try." She moved with him toward the dance floor.

She was right, she decided as they danced to the slow jazz beat of "Stormy Weather." Every inch of her yearned toward Blake. He felt too good, his arms were too right, the fit of his hips against hers was too perfect. Dancing this way should be declared a bedroom activity.

She leaned her head against his shoulder. She would have this evening and tomorrow. After that he would be gone and all her tomorrows would be empty. The words of the song seemed written just for her. It kept rainin' all the time.

Jessie wondered if leaving on The Joy Bus would stop the rain.

Five

Jessie looked at the clock. Four A.M. Flinging the covers aside, she got out of bed. There was no use trying to sleep. The music of the ball was still singing through her veins. The feel of dancing in Blake's arms wouldn't go away.

She stuck her feet into high-heeled mules and paced the floor. What was she going to do? she wondered. Blake would be going soon, and she longed to go with him. The attraction of freedom was strong, but the influence of her past was even stronger.

She wore an impatient path in the carpet, but no answers came. She was torn between going and staying. There was only one person she could talk to about her problem—Hunter. She flung open her door and went straight to his bedroom.

Tapping sharply on the door, she called, "Hunter."

"Jessie, is that you?" His voice was muffled.

"Yes." She walked in without waiting for an invitation. "Scoot over, I need to talk to you."

Yawning hugely, Hunter sat up, pulling the sheet

around his bare chest, and patted the bed. "Make yourself comfortable." He didn't blink an eye when she kicked off her slippers and joined him on the bed. Late night conversations weren't unusual for them. When Jessie had a problem, she wanted it solved immediately. If she couldn't do it by herself, she always sought Hunter. Sometimes she called him at midnight and talked for a couple of hours.

"I'm so glad you're here, Hunter."

"So am I, Jessie." He reached for his robe and handed it to her. "Here. Put this on."

"Why?"

"That gown you're wearing could start a revolution. There's no use playing with fire."

Laughing, she put on the robe. "This is your old pal, Jessie. You don't have to keep up the playboy act with me."

"Just habit, I guess." He propped a pillow behind his back and leaned against the headboard. "Now, tell me what's on your mind."

"Blake."

"I thought so."

"I can't get him out of my head."

"Jessie, have you ever thought that maybe you shouldn't even try? Maybe it's time to risk loving again."

"I'm scared."

He reached for her hand. "I know you are, baby. Just hold on for a minute."

They sat on the bed side by side, two good friends who took their strength from each other. Jessie held Hunter's hand, not saying anything, until his great tranquillity began to seep into her. At last she let go of his hand.

"Thanks, Hunter."

"Anytime, Jessie."

"I don't want to make another mistake."

"Everybody makes mistakes."

"When it comes to men, I seem to make more than my share of wrong choices."

"Twice. That's not such a bad track record. It's time to put all that behind you."

"The engagement to Harry was nothing but a rebound."

"I tried to tell you that at the time."

"I know. That's all behind me. I can even laugh about it now, all the gossip in the powder room, the raised eyebrows, the talk about Jessie Wentworth's unfortunate choice of men."

"It's still Rick, isn't it?"

"Yes. I should have known Hunter. I should have *known*."

"You were young. You thought you were in love."

"Sometimes—when I think about him, about us together—I still believe it was love. How do you know the difference, Hunter? How do you separate lust from love? How do you know that the man of your dreams isn't going to turn into ashes in a month or a year, or even ten years?"

"Jessie, if I knew the answers to all your questions I'd be the richest man in Dallas."

"You already are."

"How could I forget? That scandalous bunny nearly raped me on the dance floor when she found out about my toys."

Jessie threw back her head and laughed with delight. "You're turning into a naughty old man."

"Maybe love would be my redemption. Mrs. Jones thinks so."

Jessie became solemn. "Will you still be my best friend after you fall in love?"

"You can count on me." He studied the expression on her face. "I think you should go with Blake."

"Why?"

"Consider your options. If you stay here, you risk losing a good man and maybe the best chance in your life for happiness. If you go, the most you can lose is a few weeks work and perhaps your temper if he turns out to be a mistake. I ran a check on him. He passed with flying colors." He patted her hand. "One of the reasons I admire you is that you've always been willing to take a risk. I think that's why you're such a successful businesswoman. Go for it, Jessie."

She leaned over and kissed his cheek. "Thanks, Hunter. Maybe I will." She stood up and shucked his robe. "Good night."

" 'Night, Jessie." He was asleep before she even left the room.

Two days later, Jessie began to have second thoughts about her decision as she watched Blake load his animals onto The Joy Bus. She was standing on the flagstone veranda beside Hunter.

"I forgot about the wretched rabbits," she said.

"You're not going to back out now, are you, Jessie?" Hunter asked.

"Not on your life. This is one risk I'm going to take."

"Good girl."

"Besides, there's that crazy bet we made."

Blake overheard her comment as he walked toward them. "I wouldn't term the bet crazy." He reached up and pulled a silver dollar from behind Jessie's ear. Taking her hand, he pressed it into her palm. "I'd call it magic. Ready to go, Jessie?"

The hard coin felt like a promise against her

palm. She smiled. "Ready." Turning around, she folded Hunter into a bear hug. "Good-bye, old friend. Wish me luck."

He kissed the top of her head. "You don't need luck, Jessie. You make your own."

He stepped back and watched Blake and Jessie board the bus, then he went back inside the house, whistling.

Mrs. Jones looked up from the mail she was sorting. "This is it, Hunter. I feel it in my bones. This is Jessie's big chance."

"That Blake's one hell of a lucky man."

They both went to the window and watched until The Joy Bus was out of sight.

The old bus had been completely refurbished to suit Blake's needs. A small bathroom had been added at the back. A curtained-off area contained a cot and a rod for hanging clothes. In front of that was a space for his props and animals. There were wicker baskets for Sandy and the rabbits, and small cages for the doves. The seat opposite the driver had been left intact, and the others had been torn out to accommodate a folding card table and chairs. A hot plate and a coffee pot sat on the table. The bus had a heating and cooling system fashioned after those in expensive recreational vehicles.

Jessie slipped her fur from her shoulders and tried to make herself comfortable on the seat. She realized immediately that 1950s school bus seats weren't designed for comfort; they were designed to make school children suffer. No wonder a whole generation of kids had grown up hating school, she thought. She'd buy a cushion the first chance she got.

She settled back in her seat, trying to think of cushions and comfort instead of the man at the wheel. It didn't work. Blake was a vibrant presence, a good-looking, sexy man whose vitality seemed to fill the bus. Had she made a mistake? Should she have stayed behind in Jackson where the only decisions she had to make were safe ones? Had she been temporarily blinded by his magic? Had she been conned after all?

He looked over his shoulder and smiled at her. "I'm glad you came, Jessie."

"I was just wondering whether I should have."

"Why?"

She laughed. "Your favorite question. I guess I'll have to get used to it. After all, I'm traveling with a psychology professor."

"You didn't answer my question."

She tucked her legs under her and leaned forward. "Since we'll be together the next few weeks, you might as well know. My motives aren't all that noble, and I'm not so sure that I haven't been conned."

"Maybe I did con you, Jessie. Lord knows, I would have done nearly anything to get you to come. And I can't say that my own motives are virtuous."

"Should I be scared?"

"Should I?"

They laughed together. After the laughter had subsided they were quiet for a moment, thinking their separate thoughts about unworthy motives. There was no sound in the bus except the cooing of the doves and the swish of tires on Highway 51. The next three weeks loomed ahead of them, a bright and shining jewel, a precious gift.

Blake wondered how he had ever been so lucky to land in Jessie's front yard, and she wondered what kind fate had handed Blake to her on a silver platter.

"About my motives, Jessie—I do want to show you my world. I want you to get a taste of the simple life. I want you to see people from my perspective. I want you to understand my philosophy of life."

"I want that too," she said quietly.

"But more than that, I guess I'm hoping that proximity will advance my case."

"What case is that?"

"At this point, I'm not sure. All I know, Jessie, is that I can't bear to let you go."

"That's how I feel about you, and it scares the hell out of me."

"I wish this bus would drive itself."

"So do I."

The electric silence descended on them again as the bus tires sang their harmony on the paved road.

"Don't get me wrong, Jessie," Blake finally said. "I have no intention of taking advantage of this situation. As much as you bring out the beast in me, I can still exercise some modicum of control."

"I don't know whether I'm relieved or disappointed. Being with you in this bus is likely to test my control, too. I'm a passionate woman, Blake."

He smiled. "I know. But you're curiously restrained as well. And I want to know why. I guess I'm still old-fashioned enough to believe that relationships should be built slowly, that they should be based on such stodgy old values as respect and trust and admiration."

She studied him for a moment before answering. The sincerity of his expression lent credence to his words. She hadn't made a mistake after all, she decided. He wasn't a con artist masquerading as a nice guy. He was honest and straightforward and altogether comforting. At that moment, she wanted to hug Hunter for giving her the courage to come. More than that, she wanted to hug Blake.

"If you weren't driving, I'd give you a small thank-you hug," she said.

"If you did, I'd probably wreck the bus. Your hugs have a way of disturbing me."

"Then I'll restrain myself."

"Just while I'm driving. I'll take a rain check on the hug. I've become addicted to them."

She settled back in her seat, glad that they had been honest with each other. "Where are we going?"

"Any place in particular you would like to go?"

"Don't you have an itinerary?"

"Nothing carved in stone. I worked my way northeast during the first leg of my journey and then I headed west. On the way back I took a zigzag course in order to get a cross sampling of the Southwest and the heartland of America. The general idea is to complete my research close to home, in the Deep South."

"I'm used to working with a definite schedule."

"That's what makes this journey so interesting. Some of my best research has been the result of visiting places on whim." He smiled over his shoulder at her. "You decide."

"You want me to make the choice?"

"Sure, why not? Just close your eyes and think where you'd like to be."

Jessie closed her eyes. Blake's arms. That's where she'd like to be. The thought came to her so suddenly and with such force that her eyes flew open. Lord, she hoped magicians didn't read minds.

"Natchez," she managed to say.

"Great. That's exactly the place I was thinking of."

"You don't read minds, do you?"

"No."

"Good."

"Do you have some secrets on your mind?"

"Doesn't everybody?"

"I'm good at uncovering secrets, Jessie."

"I'll consider myself forewarned." Their eyes met in the mirror, and she smiled.

"You have the most beautiful smile I've ever seen," he said. "I could write a dissertation on it."

The bus bobbed off the road while he looked at her in the mirror. He quickly turned the wheel and got the right front tire back on the pavement.

"Perhaps you should concentrate on the driving, Professor," she chided.

"I'll try. But it's not going to be easy."

They rode in companionable silence until they reached Brookhaven. Blake pulled the bus into the parking lot of a small restaurant.

"Time for lunch," he announced, "and the first road show if the restaurant owner is willing."

He was more than willing; he was delighted. And so were the patrons.

Jessie watched the transformation of their faces as Blake performed his magic. The fortyish couple who had barely spoken to each other during their meal suddenly began to carry on an animated conversation. A harried mother with her surly brood of eight relaxed so that she forgot to keep counting her children to see if they were all there. As for the children, they stopped spitting and pinching and biting one another for the duration of the show. A teenage boy stopped nervously fingering the cigarette pack in his shirt pocket, and the dour girl with him actually smiled.

After the show, Jessie watched the crowd expectantly as Blake packed up his props. But nobody came forward to thank him for the entertainment, nor to express their enjoyment, nor even to say hello.

The Joy Bus left Brookhaven behind and headed west toward Natchez.

"That was your first chance to prove me wrong," Jessie said.

"The journey has just begun."

"You'd better prepare for a week at Wentworth."

"You'd better resign yourself to a week at the University."

"Not likely."

"Wait and see."

Jessie didn't reply. She merely smiled and turned to watch the winter-barren Mississippi landscape pass by outside her window. It was dark by the time they reached Natchez.

"I think we should stay in one of those wonderful bed-and-board antebellum homes," Jessie said.

"Didn't I tell you? We'll sleep on the bus."

"Sleep on the bus!"

"Certainly. You can take the cot and I'll use my sleeping bag."

"Co-ed sleeping arrangements aren't a part of this deal."

"There's a curtain. It'll be as private as two separate hotel rooms."

"I'll take a hotel room, thank you."

"Do you know any hotels that allow a man to check in with six doves, two rabbits, and a dog?"

"Let the animals sleep in the bus."

"It's too dangerous to leave them alone. Of course, I can drop you off at a motel, but sleeping in The Joy Bus is part of the adventure. You can check into a motel any time. How many chances have you ever had to sleep in a magic bus?"

She was beginning to weaken. "You're very convincing. Has anybody ever told you that you'd make a good con artist?"

"If I remember correctly, that was your first impression of me."

"I don't know why I ever changed my mind."

"Change your mind, Jessie."

"About what?"

"Sleeping in the bus." He turned around and smiled at her. "I promise not to bite."

She wasn't altogether sure she wanted him to keep that promise. "Well, all right. But on a trial basis. If Sandy comes behind that curtain to take a bite of me while I'm sleeping, this is my last night on the bus, magic or not."

Blake reached down to scratch behind the ears of his dog, who was snuggled against his legs. "Did you hear that, Sandy? If you don't behave, we'll lose Jessie. I don't want to lose Jessie, do you?"

The way he said it made Jessie think of more than separate sleeping arrangements. She thought of futures and lifetimes and promises. Her heart was light as Blake parked the bus under a giant oak tree in a park beside the Mississippi River.

He turned to smile at her. "Here we are. Who could ask for a more perfect setting? Just look at the river outside your window. A man could be content to spend a lifetime contemplating the wonders of that river."

"You might get hungry."

He laughed. "Ever-practical Jessie."

"Hunger does that to me. Brookhaven was a long time ago, and, anyway, I didn't eat much. I was too busy looking for a grateful person."

She stood up and stretched, unaware that her move made Blake completely forget about the river. As he watched her he decided that a man could spend a lifetime contemplating the wonders of Jessie Wentworth. He wondered if she had any idea how heart-stoppingly beautiful she was. Probably not. She was spunky and aggressive and a touch aristocratic, but she didn't seem to be vain at all.

"Natchez has some really fine restaurants," she said. "Why don't we freshen up and treat ourselves?"

"I had in mind a simple meal on the bus."

Jessie suddenly realized the difference in their financial situations. She took extravagant meals for granted, but she knew that professors from Mississippi universities weren't rich.

"We didn't talk about financial arrangements before I came on this trip, Blake. I'll pick up the tab for everything while I'm with you—meals, gas, everything."

"Now, wait a minute, Jessie. Meager though my wages are, they are sufficient to cover the expenses of this trip." He smiled. "And that includes an occasional guest."

"I'm not an occasional guest: I'm a three-week boarder, and I insist on at least paying my own way."

"Jessie . . ."

"I'll take the next bus back to Jackson otherwise."

"It won't be a pink bus."

"I don't care; I'll go anyway."

"Did anybody ever tell you that you're a stubborn woman?"

"Many times. Hunter says that obstinance is my middle name."

"You've won your case, Jessie. Separate tabs. Except for tonight. You're my guest."

She started to protest again, and he reached out and put his hand over her mouth.

"Will you stop being head of the Wentworth department stores for a second and listen to me?"

Her eyes were dancing as she nodded. She was toying with the idea of biting his hand to see if it tasted as good as it felt.

It was no longer necessary for Blake to keep his hand over her mouth, but he did anyway. It made a nice substitute for kissing her, which was what he really wanted to do.

"You misunderstood my motives," he said. "Haven't you noticed what a sunshiny day we've had? That means the sunset over the river will be spectacular tonight. Where else could you eat and have such a view?"

His hand was still over her mouth. He moved closer so that he was only inches away. Jessie thought that if he took one more step she'd forget about trying to exercise control.

"I have a can of clam chowder in my cupboard that I can transform into a gourmet's delight with my magic touch. Does that sound enticing?"

His touch was magic, all right, Jessie thought, and furthermore he was enticing. She couldn't stand it a minute more without doing something. She took a small nip of his hand. It *did* taste good. If he hadn't moved it away she would have taken another.

"Jessie?" There were a dozen questions in that one word. As he looked down at her, his eyes were the turbulent gray of a winter sea.

She gave him a innocent smile. "Just testing your control. Besides, how can I answer your question with your hand over my mouth? I suppose professors are accustomed to asking rhetorical questions."

"I suppose so," he said absently, for his mind wasn't on what she had said. It was on what she had done. Her bite—with a little teeth and a lot of tongue—had been erotic. It had been an invitation that he found almost impossible to resist. He thought about taking her in his arms and putting an end to all his agony. He thought about giving her a kiss that would escalate into an affair. He wanted to pull her behind the curtain and rip aside that pink confection she called a sweater. He ached for release from the desire that raged through him.

"If you do that again," he said, "I won't be responsible for my actions."

"Sorry, Blake. I couldn't resist." She took a step away and folded her hands behind her back. "Is that better?"

"Umhmm." It was less a word than a groan. He raked his hands through his hair. "I don't want to spoil this by taking you like some sex-starved beast."

She reached out to touch his arm, then thought better of it. "Why don't we do something safe— like cook?"

"Right."

He hurried to the shelf as if demons were after him and took down a can of clam chowder. Next he pulled milk and sweet creamery butter from the small portable refrigerator.

Jessie laughed. "I thought you said you were going to use magic. Anybody can add butter."

"Wait and see."

She crossed the small space to him. "I'm going to look over your shoulder. If you use any of that abracadabra on *my* clam chowder, I want to know about it."

With Jessie standing so close, the only feat of magic Blake performed was not spilling the soup. He had to concentrate very hard to keep his mind on the butter and off the fragrance of Jessie. What was she wearing? She smelled of sunshine and sweet summer flowers. His senses reeled and he was surprised that cartoon bluebirds weren't flying around The Joy Bus.

"Chowder will be ready in a jiffy," he said. He set the pot on the hot plate and bent down to look out the window. "And just in time too. Look at that sunset."

Jessie's long, silky hair brushed his arm as she leaned down beside him.

"It's breathtaking," she said.

He turned to look at her face. "It certainly is." But he wasn't talking about the sunset.

Their gazes locked and held. For a moment they experienced a surge of recognition, as though each had found within the other an emotion they had not known was there. Their breaths mingled as they leaned closer, merely a kiss away. The air crackled with words unspoken and gestures not made. They stood there so long that the window fogged over. Behind them, the clam chowder bubbled in the pot and the doves cooed in their cages.

"Your soup's boiling," Jessie said, and the moment was gone.

Blake turned away, and she was sorry. "So it is," he said.

He took two bowls from a small cabinet, filled them with steaming chowder, and put them on the table. He pulled out a chair for Jessie.

Bowing from the waist, he said, "Allow me, mademoiselle. You are now about to embark upon the pleasure of dining at the finest French restaurant in Natchez, Chez Montgomery."

She laughed at his antics and joined in. "Oh, but, monsieur, I'm not dressed for the occasion."

"Never fear, mademoiselle. Did I not tell you that Chez Montgomery is also a magic restaurant?"

Blake left the table and donned his cape. By the time he returned, the setting sun, its light streaming in through the windows, had turned the interior of the bus to rose-gold. He stood in the glow beside Jessie's chair and waved a wand over her hair.

Jessie felt a sudden weight on her head. Reaching up, she removed a tiara. She was enchanted. The paste diamonds sparkled so in the glow of the sunset that they might have been Cartier's most expensive.

Blake took the tiara and replaced it tenderly on her head. "Magic jewels for a magical lady," he said.

Jessie's emotions were on such a rampage she was afraid to speak. Fortunately, she didn't have to. Blake waved his wand again, and a candelabrum appeared on the table. He passed his hand over the candles and they burst into flame.

Jessie clapped her hands with delight. "How did you do that?"

"Never ask a magician such a question." He removed his cape and slid into the other chair. "Is your clam chowder hot enough?"

"I wouldn't dare say no. You'd probably wave your hand over my bowl and set it on fire."

They ate their soup in the rosy glow of sunset and the golden glow of candlelight. Outside their window, the Mississippi River put on a show reserved for those who were patient enough to sit and watch. Its swirling waters, which sometimes appeared muddy and yellow in the glaring light of day, took on the jewel tones of the setting sun. Waves, whipped to whitecaps by the January wind, shimmered golden and appeared to be doing an intricate ballet. Looking out the bus window, Jessie could almost imagine that she heard the music of Tchaikovsky.

The gold gradually faded and the waters turned pink and rose and red, as if they had swallowed an enormous rainbow. Here and there purple shadows deepened, giving the mighty river a mysterious air, as if it knew something that no one else knew, as if it harbored secrets too profound to tell. And then, in its capricious January way, the sun dropped abruptly below the horizon, leaving the river a black-purple, leaving it to chart its own course in the cold night.

Jessie and Blake watched the display in awed silence. Blake felt sorry for all the underprivileged who were trapped behind four walls, dining under the glare of electric lights, and seeing nothing more spectacular than spastic posturings on a television sitcom. He glanced across the table at Jessie and was filled with contentment. He felt sorry for everyone who had not seen this particular sunset in the company of this particular woman.

Jessie stared out the window long after there wasn't anything to see. Funny how this particular sunset should give her such pleasure, she thought. It was almost as if she had never seen a sunset before. She gazed across the candle flames at Blake. What magic was he working on her? Could she spend three weeks in his company without being caught up in his wonderful world of illusion? She touched her tiara to assure herself that it was real. It was paste, not diamonds. It was a cheap imitation of the real thing, made to appear magic by sleight of hand. If she wasn't very careful, she'd find herself under a sorcerer's spell.

She spoke in order to diffuse that spell. "So that's what you meant by the simple pleasures?"

"Yes. Did it give you joy?"

The question was unexpected. How could she tell him that he was a part of the joy? The reckless bet she had made took on a new dimension. She decided to put everything back into perspective.

"I'm not won over as easily as that, Professor. If you want to convince me that joy comes from innocence, you'll have to do more than produce one sunset."

He reached across the table and took her hand. "For you, Jessie, I'd produce a thousand sunsets."

The flames from the candles shot rainbow prisms from her tiara, and Jessie was once more caught up in the magic of Dr. Blake Montgomery.

Six

Blake tried to forget that Jessie was only a few feet away from him . . . taking a bath. He bent over his journal, writing notes that sometimes made sense and sometimes didn't. Finally he threw the pen down and leaned back in his chair. Inhaling deeply, he let the fragrant steam from her bath fill his senses. What was she using in there? he wondered. A whole garden of flowers designed to drive him wild? The pink bus had become an erotic steam bath.

Sweat trickled down the side of his face and into the collar of his shirt. He rested his head on his hands and groaned. "Good Lord, I forgot about having to share a bath with her." He pictured her naked in the small tub, the water caressing her legs, lapping with familiarity at her thighs, running in sparkling paths down her breasts.

He stood up so quickly the chair fell over. "Come on, Sandy. Let's take a walk." He looked down at himself ironically. "That is, if I can walk."

The moppet dog cocked her head as if to say,

"Walk in this weather? Have you gone crazy?" But, loyal little companion that she was, she wagged her tail and bounded after him.

The cold wind coming off the river made Blake draw his jacket collar up around his ears. "The wind's a little brisk, Sandy, but it beats the torture of Jessie's bath."

Sandy barked her agreement. She was happy to get away from the woman who had intruded upon their otherwise peaceful journey.

Blake roamed the banks of the Mississippi, looking out across its night-dark waters, thinking thoughts that were much too sizzling to be construed as research. When the wind had chilled him to the bone but had done nothing to cool his overheated mind, he turned back to the bus.

"No use freezing our tails off, Sandy. I've got three more weeks of this. Might as well go back and face the music."

Squaring his shoulders like a soldier going to battle, he took a deep breath and entered the bus. He needed that deep breath. When he saw Jessie sitting at the table in her diaphanous gown and robe, he figured it was the only deep breath he would draw for the rest of the night, maybe for the rest of his life. His heart did a rapid fandango against his ribs, and in spite of the cold, a fine line of sweat beaded his brow.

She smiled at him. "There you are. I was afraid you'd left me with these rabbits." She stood up. The light from the candelabrum on the table shimmered through her gown, outlining her body with gold.

Blake's harsh breathing sounded like an overworked bellows. "I wish you hadn't done that," he said.

"What?"

"Moved. What is that thing you're wearing? It looks like it's woven of spider webs and dew."

She laughed. "This is my attempt at modesty. I usually sleep in the nude."

"Good Lord!"

He rushed to his magic props and began digging around in a trunk.

"Is anything wrong, Blake? What are you doing?"

His voice was muffled in the depths of the trunk. "I'm looking for an army blanket, or a suit of armor, or better yet, an army tank. Anything thick enough to cover you. Ah! Here it is." He straightened and thrust a thick cloth at her. "Put this on."

She held up the object. It was a bright red flannel with gold fringe around the edges.

"It has no armholes, Blake. What is it?"

He grabbed the cloth, took a kitchen knife, and made two slits.

"Now it has arms." Handing it back to Jessie, he said, "It used to be a magic tablecloth. Now it's a robe."

She studied him as she got into her makeshift robe. Every muscle in his body was bunched and tense as if he were getting ready to leap into battle.

"Blake?"

"What?"

"I didn't mean to tease you. It's just that I made my decision to come with you so late, I didn't have time to buy appropriate clothes. I packed what I had."

"It's okay, Jessie."

"Tomorrow I promise to buy something a little less . . ." She hesitated, searching for the right word.

"Explosive," he finished for her.

She laughed. "Something with buttons up to the neck and a granny collar."

"And feet and maybe a chastity belt."

"Right. After all, I didn't come with you to start an ill-timed affair. I'm here to see if your way of life is freer than mine."

"Don't forget the bet."

"How could I forget? This is the day of pop tops, remote control, and instant gratification, Blake. I don't think you'll win."

"We'll see, Jessie. Now, if you don't mind waiting out here, I'll take my bath. Tomorrow we'll talk about a schedule, establish some sort of routine."

"Let me get a book first."

She disappeared behind the curtain and returned with a mystery novel. As Blake watched her sit at the table he decided the tablecloth did nothing except add fuel to the fire. The cloth covered the back of her, but her front was now outlined with fringe that bounced in all the right places. He could write a book on the way that fringe looked nestled in her cleavage. Clenching his jaw, he beat a hasty retreat through the curtain.

He sang off-key while he bathed. Jessie closed her book and gave thanks for small favors. The man who was magic had produced a sunset designed to melt the most stubborn heart, presented a jeweled crown to bedazzle the most die-hard cynic, and capped the evening with candlelight. At least she wouldn't be further seduced by romantic ballads.

She smiled at his choice of song—"The Whiffen-poof Song"—with hilarious emphasis on "Baa, Baa, Baa." With that cacophony in the background, she considered her surroundings. The bus was small, but neat and cozy, lit by the candelabrum and a pale wafer moon. She could hear the rhythmic murmur of water against the shore outside. The doves, huddled together in fluffy gray balls, occasionally added their throaty voices to the river's song.

Wentworth Manor seemed very far away. There was no telephone to interrupt the peace; there was no huge staff to manage; there were no budgets and no meetings. The simple life, she thought. It was great. For a while, at least. She knew herself too well to believe that she could live this way forever, cloistered away from the hustle-bustle world she knew. She enjoyed challenge, even an occasional controversy. She was too restless to live forever in a cocoon of tranquillity.

When Blake came back through the curtain, she made no pretense of reading her book.

"Do you always sing when you bathe?" she asked.

"Yes. But I don't usually have an audience except the animals. And they're tone deaf."

"Good." She stood up, unaware of the fringe jiggling enticingly around her breasts. "I'm glad your singing is so terrible. Otherwise I might become mellow and sentimental and romantic and do something foolish." She lifted the curtain. "Good night, Blake."

"Good night, Jessie." He stood staring at the curtain long after it had closed behind her. A small muscle twitched in his jaw as he argued with himself. With the sunset and candlelight, it *had* been a romantic evening. He could feel its effect on Jessie. All he had to do was walk through that curtain and take her.

"Damn," he muttered. He jerked his sleeping bag off a shelf with more than necessary vigor. "I'm reacting like a stallion at stud."

Jessie stuck her head through the curtain. "Did you say something?"

"Just talking to myself. It's a habit of absent-minded professors."

He stood mesmerized again as the curtain drifted shut. Then he took off his robe, flipped open his sleeping bag, and crawled inside. All his ideas about himself threatened to crumble under the onslaught of his passion. He had always considered himself an intelligent, steady, self-controlled man. Surely he could get through the next three weeks with his self-esteem still intact. Surely he could show Jessie a simple, free life without complicating matters.

He tossed about in the bag, hopelessly tangling himself in the unaccustomed pajamas. Sleep was going to be a long time coming.

Jessie was having the same trouble. At first she tried to blame it on her bed. It was an old army cot that sagged in the middle. Then she tried blaming it on the pigeons. She wasn't accustomed to all that billing and cooing, or whatever they were doing out there. Next she thought about the rabbits. How could she ever get a decent night's sleep, she wondered, with those devious creatures only a few feet away?

Finally her basically honest nature asserted itself. She knew the trouble was the man on the other side of the curtain. Dr. Blake Montgomery had worked some kind of magic that made the past seem unimportant. In his presence, she could forget about Rick and the pain of his deception. She could put aside the old feelings of betrayal and devastation. She could pretend that he had never existed. Almost.

She sat up and banged her lumpy pillow with her fists. She had nobody to talk to. For an instant she considered talking to Blake, but that would never do. He was at the center of her dilemma.

"Damn." She sat cross-legged in her sagging bed and stared at the makeshift robe she had tossed on the floor. "What the heck," she said as she peeled off her gown and tossed it on top of the red tablecloth. She'd try anything in order to sleep.

Jessie slept late. When she emerged from behind the curtain, Blake was sitting at the table making careful notes. His research papers were spread over the table in neat stacks.

He looked up and smiled. "Good morning. Sleep well?"

"You must be joking. That cot was designed as a prehistoric torture rack."

He laughed. "I've gotten used to it. Make yourself at home. I thought I'd get an early start today, so I didn't wait breakfast on you."

"Fine. I don't want to disrupt your schedule in any way. Go right ahead with your work and don't mind me."

It was impossible not to, Blake thought. She was every man's vision of what a woman ought to be. Even the harsh sunlight pouring through the bus windows did nothing to diminish her beauty. With her black hair hanging loose in a shining mass and her face devoid of makeup, she had a particularly dewy and innocent quality. She made him want to write sonnets. She made him want to slay dragons. She made him want to lock the bus and throw away the keys and stay beside the river forever, exploring the wonders of her.

He bent over his notes. He was drunk, he decided. Drunk on love. The thought was so strong that he wondered whether he had spoken aloud. He looked up to see if Jessie had heard, but she was bending over, exploring the contents of the refrigerator.

He felt his chest tighten. He wished she wouldn't bend over like that. What was happening to him? All his carefully researched philosophies seemed to be falling like a house of cards after one night on the bus with Jessie. The three weeks that yesterday had gleamed before him like a promise now loomed like a dark shadow. He had to have some air.

"I think I'll take a walk while you finish your breakfast, Jessie." He was out the door before she could reply.

It was just as well, Jessie decided. Her wretched night on the cot was still fresh on her mind. She didn't know if she could stand being in Blake's presence one more minute without touching him. The temptation was too great. Last night had been torture, and this morning was no better. Somehow Blake, with his shining hair and high ideals, represented all that she didn't have. He represented the freedom to move through life as he pleased, unshackled by the demands of great wealth. Because of his ease with people, he represented a charming social grace that always seemed to escape her. And then there was that mystical, magical something that might be called love by the innocent, but Jessie was too sophisticated to name it anything except longings of the flesh. Still, Blake made her long in a way she hadn't known since her youth.

Was everything he represented merely illusion? Could she stay on the bus and find out without risking her heart again? Should she turn tail and run back to Jackson like a coward?

She stood in front of the refrigerator, absently holding the milk jug, searching her mind for answers to the questions that beset her. She was determined not to add a third mistake to her list. Granted, those two wrong choices had been made a long time ago, but she didn't want to make another. She had a good life, work she enjoyed, loving parents, enough financial security to last a lifetime. But something was missing, and she had seen that something in Blake. Not just the sexual attraction, but the freedom, the simple joy of his life-style.

She closed the refrigerator door and poured milk over her cereal. This time, she would be absolutely sure, she decided. She wouldn't let lust get in the way of common sense. She would get the priorities right. What had Blake said about relationships? They were built on old-fashioned values. This time she would look for the values before she committed her heart.

"After all, I'm not nineteen anymore."

She didn't realize she had spoken aloud until Sandy growled at her.

"Could I bribe you with a tidbit, you little devil?"

She reached for the box of dog biscuits and offered one to Sandy. The little dog looked almost human as she lifted her nose disdainfully and turned her back on Jessie.

"Okay, if that's the way you want to be." She put the biscuit on the floor near Sandy. "If you change your mind, here it is. And furthermore, I want you to know that putting this biscuit on the floor is an act of supreme courage and bravery on my part, considering that George and Floyd are sitting in their bunny baskets thinking up evil schemes."

After breakfast Jessie stalked around the bus, wondering what was keeping Blake. Her nerves were taut from the nearly sleepless night, and

America's most popular, most compelling romance novels...

Here, at last...love stories that really involve you! Fresh, finely crafted novels with story lines so believable you'll feel you're actually living them! Characters you can relate to...exciting places to visit...unexpected plot twists...all in all, exciting romances that satisfy your mind and delight your heart.

Now you can be sure you'll never, ever miss a single Loveswept title by enrolling in our special reader's home delivery service. A service that will bring all four new Loveswept romances published every month into your home—and deliver them to you before they appear in the bookstores!

Examine 4 Loveswept Novels for

15 days FREE!

(SEE OTHER SIDE FOR DETAILS)

America's most popular, most compelling romance novels...

Here, at last...love stories that really involve you! Fresh, finely crafted novels with story lines so believable you'll feel you're actually living them! Characters you can relate to...exciting places to visit...unexpected plot twists...all in all, exciting romances that satisfy your mind and delight your heart.

EXAMINE 4 LOVESWEPT NOVELS FOR

15 Days FREE!

To introduce you to this fabulous service, you'll get four brand-new Loveswept releases not yet in the bookstores. These four exciting new titles are yours to examine for 15 days without obligation to buy. Keep them if you wish for just $9.95 plus postage and handling and any applicable sales tax.

☐ **YES,** please send me four new romances for a 15-day FREE examination. If I keep them, I will pay just $9.95 plus postage and handling and any applicable sales tax and you will enter my name on your preferred customer list to receive all four new Loveswept novels published each month *before* they are released to the bookstores—always on the same 15-day free examination basis.

20123

Name_____

Address_____

City_____

State_____Zip_____

My Guarantee: I am never required to buy any shipment unless I wish. I may preview each shipment for 15 days. If I don't want it, I simply return the shipment within 15 days and owe nothing for it.

R 123

Now you can be sure you'll never, ever miss a single Loveswept title by enrolling in our special reader's home delivery service. A service that will bring all four new Loveswept romances published every month into your home—and deliver them to you before they appear in the bookstores!

Examine 4 Loveswept Novels for

15 days FREE!

(SEE OTHER SIDE FOR DETAILS)

quite suddenly she realized that she was facing three weeks of confinement with Blake. Yesterday's beautiful gift became an enormous problem. Not only was there the task of keeping the attraction in perspective, but also there was the matter of time. Too much time with too little to do. Jessie had always been an active woman. Her days were filled with business challenges. What on earth was she to do for three weeks in this pink bus? Hunter had said "Take a vacation." Heck, she hadn't had a vacation in so long she didn't know what to do with one.

She whirled through the curtain and unpacked her bags. The clothes rod was totally inadequate for all her clothes. Whatever would she do without a maid? she wondered as she piled her blouses and skirts and slacks in every available corner. She could organize budget reports and financial statements and departmental reports with the greatest of ease, but domesticity was alien to her. After thirty minutes of trying to arrange too many clothes into too little space, she was floundering in a brightly colored sea of wool and silk and satin.

She was standing in the middle of the bus looking for a place to put her lingerie when Blake returned.

It was not a good time for him to see his bus looking as if it had been struck by a hurricane. He looked from the dirty breakfast dishes on the table to the clothes strewn around the bus to the gorgeous woman who was the current cause of his agony.

"What's going on here?"

"I'm unpacking."

"You brought all *that*"—he waved his arm to encompass the mounds of clothes—"for a three-week trip?" Too late, he realized he had snapped at her. But, dammit, he supposed he had a reason to snap. He was cold from his walk, and his nerves were jangled from lack of sleep. Furthermore, seeing Jessie standing there holding a wisp of panties in her hands made him feel such a surge of desire that he had to snap or go crazy.

She took immediate offense. "You didn't expect me to make this trip naked, did you?"

It was a poor choice of words. He became even more inflamed. "Dammit, Jessie, we're traveling in a school bus, not a resort hotel."

"It certainly isn't! That tub is barely big enough for my foot, let alone all of me. There's no place to put my clothes, not to mention my personal items. And that primitive cot is enough to make a saint cuss."

Their emotions, already raw with restrained passion, got completely out of control. They glared at each other across the small space that separated them.

"I didn't hear you complaining last night," he said.

"That's because I'm too mannerly."

"Well, what happened to all those manners when it came time to wash your breakfast dishes?"

"Washing dishes never occurred to me."

He stalked around her and put the milk in the refrigerator. "I suppose it never occurred to you that the milk would sour."

"How can you stand there talking about sour milk when I don't even have a place to put my underwear?"

"I suppose a carton of sour milk is nothing to you?"

"We can buy more."

As he faced her, some of his earlier rage began

to leave. The real issue was not a carton of sour milk, and he knew it. The real issue was not even the scattered clothes. His voice was softer when he spoke again.

"You can fix everything with money, can't you, Jessie?"

Stung by his accusation, she flung her panties in his face. He caught them with one hand and crammed them into his pocket.

"*You're* the one who wanted me to come," she yelled.

"Nobody made you."

"I must have been out of my mind."

Their faces were stiff with hurt and anger as they continued to glare at each other. Suddenly, Jessie crumbled. She lifted a trembling hand and pushed back her hair.

"What did you expect of me, Blake? Did you think I'd become domestic the minute I stepped aboard this bus? I'm used to cooks and house-keepers and maids. I can't be somebody else simply because you want me to be. I'm accustomed to all the luxuries that wealth affords. You can't change that."

He closed the space between them and pulled her into his arms. "I'm sorry, Jessie. Lord, I'm sorry."

He attempted to cradle her head on his shoulder, but she remained rigid and unyielding.

"Please. Don't make matters worse, Blake."

He released her and took a step back. "I won't try to make excuses for losing control like that. There are none."

She looked around the bus at her scattered possessions and smiled weakly. "Yes, there are. I'm accustomed to running a tight ship in my business. I should have known you'd have a system, and I should have been prepared to live by it."

"How could you live by my rules if I never explained them to you? This is a situation that never should have happened, Jessie, and I take full responsibility."

"Forget it. I'm a grown woman. There are a few things I should have figured out by myself."

"Jessie." He held out a tentative hand and then drew it back. "I'm going to help you straighten all this up, then I'm going to call a taxi on that pay phone in the park and go into town. I have to arrange a magic show."

"Leave. Go now."

"No. I don't want to leave you like this."

"I need to be by myself. Please go."

He gave her a long look, a look filled with all the things he didn't say. A look that said "I'm confused too. I'm half in love and don't know why, and I'd rather cut off my right hand than hurt you. Forgive me." He reached into his pocket and pulled out a small object.

"Hold out your hand, Jessie."

She obeyed, and he pressed a key into her palm.

"A key to the bus," he said. "I meant to give it to you yesterday. If you need to leave, lock up."

And then he was gone.

Jessie sat down cross-legged in the middle of her mess and rested her head on her hands. It was a dejected position, as if she were in mourning. But she wasn't mourning. Far from it. She was devising a plan. She sat quietly for such a long time that Sandy's curiosity overcame her hatred. The little dog crept up and nudged Jessie's knee.

Automatically, Jessie reached out and patted

the small head. "They say you can't teach an old dog new tricks. We'll see about that."

Squaring her shoulders and jutting out her chin, she put her plan into action.

While Jessie was plotting and planning, Blake was lurching toward town in a taxi that could barely move with a taxi driver who rarely shut up.

"You're new in town, ain't you?" The taxi driver looked at Blake in the rearview mirror.

"Yes." Ordinarily Blake would have enjoyed conversing with the man, but he was still trying to analyze the fight with Jessie and wondering how two intelligent people could allow something like that to happen.

The cab driver didn't let Blake's short reply deter him. Pushing his greasy cap back off a pockmarked forehead, he launched into his standard travelogue. "Well, I'll tell you, there ain't much doin' this time of year, 'less you like highbrow stuff, simp-phonies and such, but we got some mighty pretty houses." He eased the wheezing old cab around a corner. "Yessir, them anti-bell houses is somethin' to be proud of. Just goes to show that when it comes to culture, we got it all over them Yankees." He stopped talking long enough to spit a stream of tobacco into a tin can at his feet. "This here's the oldest city along the Miss'sippi River. If that ain't somethin' to brag about, I don't know what is." He twisted his head around to see the effect of his speech on his passenger. Earl considered himself to be the resident expert on local history. Never mind fancy folks with fancy university degrees. He wanted to see if his passenger was showing the proper awe.

Although Blake hadn't been paying much attention to the monologue, he realized that a response was required. "That's interesting." He figured he had covered all bases with his reply.

It wasn't the effusive sort of reply Earl had expected, but it would do. "Say, ain't I seen you somewhere? You look like one of them movin' pitchure stars that sells hair tonic on the teevee."

Blake suppressed his smile. "No, I'm afraid not. I'm a simple psychology professor. I'm on sabbatical doing research for a book."

Earl beamed. He didn't know what sabbatical was, but he considered himself to be quite a psychologist, what with his everyday dealings with people, and he knew about books. Books, if they were scandalous enough, went on to become movies. "If you ever need any material for that book," he said, "come to me. The things I've heard in this here cab would make a 3-D X-rated, pot-boilin', gut-bustin' movie. Me and you could get rich off'n what I know." He was so excited by the prospect that he swerved the cab and nearly knocked down old Mrs. Pennypacker, who was trying to cross the street.

"Watch out!" Blake said.

Earl spat a stream of tobacco. "Snobby old biddy. Ought to watch where she's goin'. Always jay-walkin', gettin' honest folks in trouble."

Blake didn't realize he was on the edge of his seat until they turned a corner and left Mrs. Pennypacker behind. As he sat back for the rest of the ride, he figured that two good things had come out of the incident: the cab driver didn't mention the scandalous movie again, and he had forgotten about his fight with Jessie. It was time to stop mulling over what had already happened and make plans for amends. He would push his passion aside and treat her with the same casual interest he had for all his guests. He wouldn't let the trip get bogged down with unproductive emotions. He would keep sight of his primary goal: proving his philosophy to her. He would—

"Here we are, Professor." The cab driver interrupted his thoughts. "That'll be six-twenty."

Absentmindedly Blake reached into his pocket and pulled out a wad of bills. To his chagrin, Jessie's lace panties came with them.

Earl laughed so hard he showed two gold molars in the back of his mouth. "Danged if I've ever had anybody try to pay me in women's underwear before."

It was one of the few times in his life that Blake was speechless. He stared from the panties to the cab driver. Finally the humor of the situation struck him, and he chuckled.

"It's not what you think. You see—" He stopped. He couldn't explain why he had the panties in his pocket without telling about his fight with Jessie. And he would never do that. "I'm a magician," he finished lamely.

Earl burst into another fit of laughing. "Lord a' mercy, that's a new one. I'll have to remember that next time my wife catches me red-handed with some other woman's drawers." He thumped his knee with renewed delight. "Magic. Wait'll I tell the boys down at the station."

Earl was having such a good laugh, Blake didn't disillusion him with the truth. Stuffing the panties back into his pocket, he paid the cab fare and left to arrange a magic show.

It was late when he returned to The Joy Bus. Making the arrangements for the show had taken a while, and his reluctance to face Jessie again had made him dawdle away a good part of the day. As he pushed open the door of the bus, he tried to decide whether his reluctance was due to guilt or fear. He felt guilty about this morning's quarrel. Although he knew it hadn't been solely his fault, he believed he should have handled the situation better. The fear—a virtual stranger to him—was harder to analyze. It had many faces and many names. Since meeting Jessie, he had discovered within himself a beast of desire that was hard to control. He was afraid of pushing her too fast, too hard. He was afraid of emphasizing their differences rather than bridging the gap.

If he ever needed to perform a feat of magic, he decided, it was now. Squaring his shoulders, he stepped inside the bus.

"Surprise!" Jessie, with a smile as polished and gleaming as her ebony hair, stepped forward to greet him.

Blake looked from her shining face to the strange interior of his old bus. Gone was the faded old sheet that had hung between the sleeping and eating areas. In its place hung a heavy beige drape on a fancy brass rod. The cover on the passenger's seat, with its patched and frayed edges, had been replaced by a handsome rust and beige plaid in plush material so thick a small mouse could get lost in it. New curtains to match the drape hung at the windows.

"Jessie, what is all this?"

"After you left, I thought about what you had said. You were right, of course. Naturally I have to learn to live in your surroundings. But that doesn't mean I can't improve them." She swept her hand around the refurbished bus. "Getting it all done today took some persuasion on my part, but I wanted to do it as a goodwill gesture."

"It's amazing, the way money talks." The instant he said it, her face changed. Her smile faded, and the glow went out of her eyes. Blake could have bitten off his tongue.

"You don't like it," she said. It was a statement rather than a question. "I'm afraid even to tell you about the cot."

From the way she had changed his curtains and his seat covers, he wouldn't have been surprised if she'd said there was a four-poster bed in the sleeping area. He'd felt comfortable with that old sheet and the mouse-eaten seat covers. Coming into The Joy Bus had been like putting on a favorite pair of worn-out bedroom slippers. He opened his mouth to tell her so, but the look on her face stopped him. To hell with the truth. He'd spin a thousand lies if he could bring the light back into her face.

"I like it, Jessie." He sat on the passenger seat and rubbed his hand over the lush pile to show how much he meant the words. To his surprise, the newly covered seat *did* feel good. "I probably would have done this myself if I'd thought about it." He smiled up at her. "But you've done it with much more élan than I would have."

She knew he was lying. "I'm a woman of action, Blake. After I had cleared away my own belongings, I took liberties with yours."

He looked at the proud tilt of her head, the clear green challenge in her eyes, and he was affected as only a man in love could be.

"You can take liberties with my belongings anytime, Jessie."

The deepened timbre of his voice and the smoldering look in his eyes quickened Jessie's heart. Its thunder crashed in her ears and reverberated through her body. The raw power of the emotion made her so weak, she had to sit down. She sank beside Blake on the passenger seat, being careful not to let herself touch him. She knew that touching him meant the end of control.

"I might as well get the full benefit of my latest mistake," she said. Even with a small space separating them, she felt as if she were drowning in the sexual energy emanating from Blake. He made no move to touch her, and yet she felt as if his hands had slid over her in heady exploration. As she looked up at him, a flame leaped in his eyes, bridged the space between them, and sent a burst of warmth through her veins.

"It was no mistake, Jessie. I accept your redecorating in the generous spirit in which it was given."

"There's no need to pretty it up with fancy words, Blake. Maybe it was selfish. Maybe I'm so accustomed to fancy surroundings that I couldn't endure the sight of that ratty old bedsheet hanging there one minute longer." She started to put her hand on his knee, then thought better of it. "Whatever it was, accept it as a truce."

"A truce. And a new beginning."

She cocked an eyebrow at him. "Is there such a thing?"

"Of course. We did it once before. Remember?"

She recalled their first meeting, their first exchange of heated words. Then she remembered his smile, the way it had beguiled her, the way it had made her forget everything except the man who owned it.

Smiling, she repeated the words he had used that day. "Let's start over."

"Agreed." He caught her hand and stood up, bringing her with him. "All good pacts are sealed in a proper manner." He inclined his head toward her as if he meant to kiss her.

Hastily, she whirled out of his grip and walked

to the small refrigerator. Bending down, she took out a bottle of wine.

"I've had this chilling. I think it would be a much safer way to seal a pact."

"But not nearly as much fun."

She pulled the cork out while he took down two glasses.

"You're the one who said relationships should be built slowly," she said.

"Foiled by my own words."

"We have three weeks." She poured the wine.

Lifting his glass, Blake said, "To the next three weeks."

Their eyes locked over the wineglasses, and suddenly the three weeks that lay ahead of them were once more a wide and sparkling vista, radiant with promise.

Seven

The new cot didn't sag in the middle, but Jessie still couldn't sleep. If only Hunter were here, she thought. With sudden decision, she got out of bed, put on her robe, and parted the curtains.

"Blake?"

"Come in, Jessie."

His voice was so alert that she wondered if he, too, had been having trouble sleeping. She stood in the doorway looking down at him. He was sitting up in his sleeping bag. The moon provided enough light to illuminate his face. Under the tousled hair, it was calm and untroubled. There was tenderness in his face, too, and understanding. It was the face of a man she could trust.

"I need a friend," she said.

"Come." He patted the sleeping bag. "I'm glad you came to me."

Tucking her new flannel gown and robe under her legs, she sat on the end of the bag.

"I don't like what happened to us today," she said.

"Neither do I. Let's do something about it."

"Today made me feel as if we inhabited different planets. I don't want to feel that far apart from you, and yet I can't seem to touch you without wanting you." Her green eyes were troubled as she looked at him. "I'm not ready for that."

"I know, Jessie. Do you want to tell me why?"

"I don't want to, but I must. It's a part of my past that is extremely painful, but I feel the time has come to deal with it openly. I like you, Blake." His eyes brightened until they seemed like gray crystals in the moonlight. The look he gave her was so intense it felt as if it penetrated her very soul. "More than like you," she murmured. "I think you're someone I could love, but my past is standing between us."

"I've felt that." He reached for her hands. "You're cold as ice. Come up here." He pulled her into the circle of his arms and smiled down at her. "Just one friend warming another."

"Are you sure?"

"The granny gown helps." He tucked her robe around her feet. "I've known about your broken engagement for a long time," he said, hoping it would make her confession easier.

"Mrs. Jones?"

"Yes."

Jessie laughed. "She tells everybody about it. She seems to think a broken engagement gives a woman an air of mystery. Mrs. Jones is an incurable romantic."

"You can laugh about it. That's a good sign."

"Of course, I can. Dear old Harry, the rotten cad, has nothing to do with my hesitation to—" She stopped.

"Fall in love?"

"Not exactly." She looked up at him. His gaze

made her feel as if she had walked into a warm room, lit by the sun and sparkling with rainbows. "I don't know. Let's just say, make a commitment."

"All right. A safe enough word. So Harry . . ."

"Webster. Harold Evans Webster, fourth-generation, blue-blooded, certified ass."

Blake laughed. "He had to be. Any man who left you would qualify for that dubious honor."

"Harry was a rebound, a way to salvage what was left of my self-esteem, a way to validate my own sexuality." She looked at the sleeping animals without really seeing them. In her mind's eye, she was seeing herself as a nineteen-year-old girl, starry-eyed and innocent, very much in love with an idealistic, poetic young man named Richard Lockhart Gainsville.

"Everybody called him Rick." Her voice was soft, far away. "We were both at Harvard. We were young and full of ideals. It was a time in our lives when the whole universe seemed to be waiting breathlessly for us to come forward and make our mark. I was going to rock the business world with my innovative ideas, and he was going to write poetry so astonishing that the literary world would never be the same."

She stopped talking as her mind traveled back in time once more. Even after all these years she could still remember the pale translucence of his skin, the way it seemed to absorb light, to invite a wondering touch.

Blake was quiet, waiting for her to continue. It was a comforting silence, a silence that reassured Jessie that he was interested. A silence that did not judge.

"I remember the night he proposed," she said. "It was the fall of my sophomore year. October. A group of us had gone to the Cape for the weekend. We rented a cabin by the ocean. The others had gone to the beach to build a bonfire. Rick and I stayed behind." As the memories crowded in on her, her voice became breathless, her speech disjointed. "There was an open fire . . . so cozy . . . he was reading . . . Poe, I think, 'Ulalume' . . . I sat beside him . . . his hand felt so right, so romantic . . . he called me his dream, his inspiration . . . I bent over . . . kissed his cheek . . . he asked me to marry him."

Blake caressed her arm, her shoulder. His touch was tender, reassuring.

"I'm here," he said.

And she knew that he was. Not as a lover, not as a judge, but as her friend. She turned her head and smiled at him.

"Thank you, Blake. Exorcising ghosts is harder than I thought it would be."

"It takes courage to deal with pain. You're doing fine, Jessie."

"We didn't wait to tell anyone," she continued. "We thought an elopement would be romantic. There was no time for a honeymoon. We rented a small apartment near the school. At first I thought his lack of passion was shyness. He said he was being considerate of me, of my 'gentle sensibilities.' I assured him that my sensibilities weren't gentle. I even told him that I was going to turn into a screaming maniac if he delayed a proper wedding night one more minute." She was quiet for a moment, gathering her courage for the rest of the story.

Blake tightened his hold on her. A great ball of rage twisted inside his chest. He wanted to smash the boy who had put his passionate Jessie through such hell. His own thoughts shocked him. He wasn't a violent man. He had always believed intelligent people could do without violence.

"I'm sorry, Jessie," he said quietly.

"I endured the private torture of my marriage for three months. Three *months*. When I think about it now, I wonder how I could have been so foolish. I wonder why I didn't leave after the first week."

"You were young."

"And naive. Finally, I realized the enormity of my mistake. Daddy came up and arranged for an annulment. But that didn't stop the humiliation. I felt totally betrayed. Not only did I lose faith in men, I lost faith in my ability to make choices. I left school and traveled in Europe for nearly a year. When I came back, I went straight into Wentworth Enterprises. It was my salvation."

She hadn't realized how tense she had been until after she finished the story. Suddenly she relaxed against Blake's shoulder, thinking how good it was to have him for a friend.

"Better?" he asked, smiling down at her.

"Yes. Until this moment, I hadn't realized how heavy ghosts can be to carry." She moved out of his arms and faced him. Her exotic eyes gleamed with courage and something like a challenge as she slanted a look at him. "I don't want your pity, Blake."

He threw back his head and laughed. "My dear Jessie, it never crossed my mind to pity you. I pity the next poor fool who tampers with your heart."

"Nobody is going to tamper with my heart again, Blake. I've made two mistakes; I don't intend to make a third."

"I stand forewarned." Abruptly, he put the teasing aside and took her hand. "I'm glad you told me. It explains a lot of things. With the past behind you, perhaps we can start anew."

She laughed. "How many times are we going to start over?"

"As many as it takes to get it right."

His smile was the magic that made her believe his words. Starting over, she thought. That was what she wanted to do. But not with haste, not as lovers.

"I feel such passion for you, Blake, that it has made me a little crazy."

"Me, too, Jessie."

"But I wanted you to know why I cannot, *will not*, rush into anything."

"I understand." He kissed her hand, then grinned. "That sexless gown should help a lot."

"You're as bad as Hunter."

"You're laughing, Jessie. That's what I wanted you to do." He placed her hand carefully back on her lap. "Now. I suggest that we be friends, good friends . . ."

"Hugging friends? I like to be touched."

"Yes." He gave her an exuberant demonstration.

"But not that tight. Lord, you have the chest of a bear."

"A friendly bear."

"As opposed to sexy."

"I'm not sure my ego can stand that."

"I think you'll bear up. Good night, best friend. After Hunter, of course."

"How you dash my ego! Good night, punster."

Peace reigned on the bus once more. In their new status as friends, Jessie and Blake found much to laugh about. She laughed at his singing and he laughed at her cooking. He laughed at her sexless granny gowns, which he privately thought weren't sexless at all, and she laughed at his 1960 vintage bathrobe, which she privately thought emphasized that fabulous chest he was striving to hide. They laughed in exhilaration at each new sunset, which seemed to have been designed especially for their pleasure.

His first magic show was a roaring success, with not one, but two grateful people coming forward to thank him afterward. Both Jessie and Blake talked of moving on, but they were reluctant to leave the river, for they had become friends here, had shared laughter and pain, had learned how to live in the harmony that only nature can teach. The river had seduced them with its flashy displays at sunset, beguiled them with its morning brilliance, lulled them with its haunting night song, and taught them with its steadfast flow toward the gulf. It was the mighty Mississippi, mysterious and timeless, and they were irrevocably bound to it.

Sandy, whose enmity toward Jessie was well known, had been won over by the matter of the dog biscuit. But she still felt obliged to put up an offended front. She hid her face in her paws every morning when Jessie came through the curtain, but Blake noticed that she kept one ear cocked for their conversation and risked peeks at Jessie every so often. Jessie offered her dog biscuits, but was repeatedly rebuffed. At Blake's suggestion, she started leaving a biscuit on the floor within Sandy's reach each morning. The little dog disdained the food until she thought no one was looking. Then she dragged it toward her blanket with a dainty paw and hid it until she could enjoy it in private.

Blake and Jessie took great delight in beating

her at her own game. One morning they made a great to-do of leaving. Then they rushed around the bus and came through the back door. They surprised Sandy in the act of eating the rejected biscuit. She looked almost human in her sheepish guilt. Blake and Jessie had a great laugh over the incident, and Sandy, having no further reason to pretend aloofness, became Jessie's staunch friend.

The interior of the bus was softly lit by the fading rays of a setting sun. Outside the windows, the Mississippi sang its ceaseless song.

Blake was teaching Jessie a few magic tricks. Sandy kept getting in the way, weaving through their legs, thumping her tail on their shoes, and licking their hands every chance she got. Blake finally picked up the little dog and put her in her basket. "If you could only do as well with befriending the rabbits," he said to Jessie.

"I don't want to befriend the rabbits. We have a long history of enmity."

"You can't learn magic if you don't reconcile yourself to George and Floyd."

"Can't I use something besides rabbits in the hat?"

"Every self-respecting magician uses rabbits."

"I'll endure the humiliation."

"Jessie . . ."

"Stop pushing, Blake, and teach me the damned trick."

"You're a stubborn woman."

"You're a persistent man. Must you always be the psychologist?"

"I can't change what I am, Jessie."

"Nor can I."

Blake realized that they were again facing each other across a chasm that separated their worlds. He was the first to bridge the gap.

"All right," he said. "No more of that. Hold the cards like this." He demonstrated.

Jessie's imitation was less than perfect.

"No," Blake said, putting his hands over hers. "Like this."

It was the first time they had touched since the night of her confession. Suddenly the cards fluttered to the floor, and they were in each other's arms. His lips were on hers and her arms were around his neck. His tongue plundered. She melted. He hauled her hips in. She arched. He swayed. She followed. He became rigid. She blossomed.

They stood together in the pink glow of sunset, swaying and arching with the passion that shook them. His hands were under her sweater, tracing her warm back. Her hands were inside his shirt, caressing his chest, curling through the springy golden hairs.

His hands moved, took the hem of her sweater, began to strip it upward.

"No," she whispered. She reeled back from his embrace. "No," she said with more conviction. "I'm not ready for this."

Blake studied her troubled face. Gently he pulled her sweater back down and smoothed it into place.

"I think it's time to move on, Jessie. The river has lulled me into thinking we could live like this forever. Just the two of us."

"I almost wish we could, Blake. But almost isn't good enough, is it?"

"No." He bent to retrieve the scattered cards. "The magic will have to wait."

• • •

That night Jessie dreamed. She dreamed that magic cards were falling on her, spades and diamonds and hearts and clubs, covering her, smothering her. She couldn't breathe, couldn't push them off. Then suddenly she didn't want to push them off. They felt warm and gentle and somehow erotic. They felt like Blake's hands.

She reached out, closed her hands around her dream vision. So soft. So warm. So furry. A warning bell sounded deep in her subconscious mind. She struggled out of the dream world. Her half-drugged mind slowly allowed reality to creep in.

Jessie screamed.

"Jessie!" Blake jerked out of his sleeping bag and kicked it aside. In his haste to get to her, he tangled the heavy new curtains around his arms. Impatiently, he ripped them off the brass rod. He glanced quickly around the small space for intruders, but saw nothing except the terrified woman. Crossing the space with two giant strides, he scooped Jessie into his arms.

She clung to him, burying her face in his shoulder.

He stroked her hair, her neck, her back. "Jessie, what's wrong?"

"The rabbits." Her voice was muffled against his shoulder.

"The what?"

She lifted her head and looked up at him. "The rabbits. I was dreaming and then they were here, on the cot." Excitement made her voice rise. "I touched them."

Blake glanced around for the culprits. They had taken refuge on Jessie's fur coat. They were huddled together, their noses twitching in fear.

"It's all right, boys," he told them.

Jessie sat up and pounded her fists on the cot.

"Never mind the wretched rabbits. What about me? They scared me half to death."

"Come here." He pulled her back into his arms and caressed her rigid back. "I'm sorry, Jessie. Sometimes the rabbits wander around at night. Knowing how you feel about them, I should have warned you." He continued gentling her with his hands. "They would never have hurt you. They're harmless little creatures. I wish I could help you understand."

She leaned against him, letting his hands soothe her fears and calm her nerves. He felt so solid, she thought, so good. His arms were like a haven. At that moment she wished that he would always be there for her. She wanted to be able to run into those safe arms whenever she needed them.

She spoke without lifting her head from his shoulder. "I know the rabbits are harmless, Blake. Deep down, I know that. I had a rabbit once . . ."

He waited a moment for her to continue. When she remained silent, he asked, "Do you want to tell me about it?"

She lifted her head and smiled. "You make confessing easy."

"It's my training."

"No. It's your shoulders."

She saw the bright flame in his eyes before he pulled her head back down. "I'm always here for you, Jessie. I want to always be here for you."

It was almost as if he had read her mind, she thought. She pressed her face into him, loving the feeling of strength in him, reveling in the sense of being protected, even cherished. If she let herself, she could give in right now. She could make a total break with the past, yield to her impulses, and pull Blake down onto the cot with her. But something held her back. She suspected that with Blake nothing would be casual. If she made love to him now, she was afraid there would be no turning back. He was the kind of man who would mark her as his forever.

Reluctantly she pulled out of his arms. She wasn't ready for that kind of commitment, and she knew if she stayed there a minute longer there would be no denying the desire that had been escalating since he had ripped down the curtain and taken her in his arms.

She moved away from him, not a safe distance, but a less dangerous one. "I'll tell you about the rabbits."

"Somehow that seems second best."

"But it's safe."

He touched her hand. All that was good and kind and beautiful seemed to be in that touch. "I'm no threat to you, Jessie. Don't you know that?"

"I'm not ready to know that. I'm not ready even to think about that."

His smile was tinged with regret. "Then I'll be your friend. I'll always be your friend. But someday . . ."

She pressed her fingers to his lips. "Shhh. Don't say anything else."

He kissed her fingertips. "Then tell me, lovely Jessie. Tell me about your rabbit."

And she did. She told about Velvet, her favorite childhood pet. She told of sunshiny days in the meadow, of happy days in the formal gardens.

"And then one day he ate my boots," she said. "I had been gone all day. I suppose he was bored. When I came home, I discovered that he had shredded the tops of my favorite leather riding boots. In a fit of childish rage I picked up a magazine and spanked him. He ran away and that was the last I ever saw of him. The gardener found him in the road the next morning. He had been killed by a passing car." Her eyes were large with appeal as she looked at Blake. "I did that. I killed Velvet."

"No, you didn't. The car killed him. You can't blame yourself for an accident."

"But I did. I cried for days. Too late, I realized I could afford dozens of pairs of leather boots, but there would never be another Velvet."

"Did you talk to your parents about Velvet's death?"

"No. They were on the Costa del Sol. I had no one to talk to except the household staff. I began to hate rabbits. I hated them because they were easy to love and easy to lose."

"Life has no guarantees, Jessie. The people and the animals we love aren't automatically exempt from tragedy. To love is to risk loss. Not to love is to risk isolation."

"Living in an ivory tower?"

"Yes."

"We're not talking about rabbits anymore, are we?"

"No. We're talking about us, Jessie." He lifted her hand to his lips. "I've fallen in love with you. I love your spirit, your courage, your brains. Your smile turns me inside out. I love the way you say my name, the way you move, the way you look in the early morning when you first wake up." He turned her hand over and fitted her palm to his cheek. "I love you, Jessie, and I—"

"Blake, don't."

"Let me finish. I don't want to lose you by making demands that you aren't ready to meet." Taking both her hands, he clasped them tightly. "Good night, Beautiful Lady."

He stood up.

"Blake, don't . . ." She reached toward him, almost touching him.

"Yes?" His face was tense, his eyes alight with anticipation as he waited for her to speak.

"Don't forget the rabbits."

"All right, Jessie." He tucked Floyd and George beneath his arms and walked toward their cages.

Jessie felt a great emptiness as she watched him go. She wanted him to stay. She wanted him to read her mind.

"Blake?"

He turned around. "Yes?" Again he waited for her to say something, anything that would keep him there with her.

She looked up at the man who was magic, the man who had beguiled her, enchanted her, almost ensnared her. The silence stretched between them.

"What will we do about the curtain?" she finally asked.

Damn the curtain, he wanted to shout. But he didn't. "Tonight, we'll shut our eyes and pretend it's still there. Tomorrow I'll see if I can rehang it."

"Good night, Blake."

He didn't reply. He needed all his strength for the torturous night ahead.

They left Natchez the next day. They left the river and the park and the lovely old town, but they couldn't leave the memories. The memories sang through their minds and hearts, keeping time to the rhythmic swish of tires against the pavement.

Just outside Natchez, Blake spotted a young woman walking down the highway. He slowed the old bus and looked for a spot to pull off the road.

"You're not stopping?" Jessie asked.

"Of course. It's too cold for anybody to be out walking. Besides, it's dangerous for a woman to hitchhike. There's no telling who will pick her up if I don't."

They were close enough for Jessie to see the girl's spike heeled shoes and electric blue stockings. A tight satin skirt rode halfway up her thighs, revealing a red lace garter. A ratty old imitation fur coat was pulled up around her ears.

"She probably has a knife tucked in that garter," Jessie said.

"She probably needs a friend," Blake said as he brought the bus to a halt on the narrow shoulder. He cranked the front door open. "Hi, I'm Dr. Blake Montgomery. Need any help?"

The young woman swung around to face him, one hip cocked defiantly forward. "Not unless you're some kind of magician," she said.

He laughed. "That's exactly what I am, a magician. Do you need a lift? We're headed toward New Orleans."

"Well, hot damn." The girl slung a tattered duffle bag aboard the bus and climbed in after it. Her high heels clattered on the steps. "The name's Wanda Lou. Pleased to meet 'cha." She stuck out her hand. Her long red fingernails resembled eagle's talons.

Blake studied the young woman as he introduced her to Jessie. It was hard to tell her age because of the heavy mascara that matted her lashes and the bright red lipstick that slashed her lips. He judged her to be in her early twenties, twenty-four at the most. He also noted the defeated slump of her shoulders and the old look in her eyes.

"Where are you headed, Wanda Lou?" he asked.

He knew better than to lecture her about the dangers of hitchhiking. The best way to help her was to show friendly interest, to speak her language.

Wanda Lou scooted onto the seat beside Jessie. She didn't seem to notice how Jessie squeezed herself tightly against the side of the bus.

"Nowhere in particular. Just as far away from home as I can get." She waved her hand in the general direction of Natchez. "Nothing back there for me but heartache."

The way she said it, with a musical twang in her voice, made Blake think of a country song. He put the bus into gear and eased back onto the road. "So you're making a brand new start?"

"Yep. I been slingin' hash as far back as I can remember, tryin' to support a drunk mother and a no-count daddy. Had to drop out of school to do it. Finally I said to myself, Wanda Lou, it's time you was movin' on. Nothin's gonna change 'til you make it change." She swiveled her head and looked at Jessie with her bright blue eyes. "Don't you think that's right, Jessie? I mean, a girl's got to think of herself sometime."

Jessie didn't know how to reply to the flashy young woman who was suddenly her traveling companion. She wasn't accustomed to making conversation with casual acquaintances. Certainly not with people as unorthodox as Wanda Lou.

"Yes," she said. As conversation, it wasn't much, but it was the best she could do.

"Say, you don't talk much do you?" Wanda Lou leaned toward her. " 'Course anybody as gorgeous as you don't have to say much. Just sit around and look pretty." She reached out and fingered Jessie's soft cashmere sweater. "Bound to be rich too. That's some high-class duds. Makes your eyes look like one of them big old green stones in the jewelry store window. If I had me some money, I'd open one of them little bow-tik shops, you know that kind with all them pretty clothes with beads and spangles and such. I got a way with a needle. Everybody says so. 'You got a real gift for sewin', Wanda Lou,' they tell me. I believe everybody ought to do what's best suited to him. Makes a feller unhappy to always be doin' somethin' he don't like. Me, I got sick and tired of slingin' hash. So I said to myself, 'Wanda Lou, it's time to be movin' on.' "

She stretched her long legs out in front of her. Being warm had made her talkative. "I guess I'd 'a froze to death if you hadn't come along. 'Course truckers are pretty good about stoppin', especially for a pretty girl. They're not supposed to, but they do." She laughed unselfconsciously and fluffed her bright red hair. " 'Course, you must know more about bein' pretty than Marilyn Monroe, Jessie. Got a better figure than her too. Too much bust spoils the way a woman looks in clothes. Them lean, clean lines give a woman class. Class, that's what you got. Pure D class."

Jessie decided that Wanda Lou would be pretty if she had all the makeup scrubbed off her face and had on some decent clothes. Some of her misgivings were disappearing under the onslaught of Wanda Lou's words. Why, she's just an ordinary person, Jessie thought. She has dreams and ambitions and a philosophy. She's simply never had a chance.

With that realization, Jessie relaxed. "Do you have any of your needlework, Wanda Lou? I'd like to see it." Unconsciously, she moved closer to the young woman.

Blake saw the movement and smiled. He had hoped that Jessie's generous nature would overcome her natural distrust of the unknown. He was quiet as he guided the bus down the road, letting Jessie get her first taste of dealing with the common man.

"Well, hot damn," Wanda Lou said. "I been dyin' to show this to somebody besides my friends. Get another opinion, you know." She unzipped her duffle bag and brought out a wrinkled garment. "A high-class lady like you is bound to know about clothes." She held the dress by the shoulders and flicked her wrists. "What do you think?"

Jessie caught her breath in astonishment. The dress was white and stunningly simple with padded, bejeweled shoulders reminiscent of the forties.

"I think it's remarkable. Where did you learn to design clothes like this?"

"Granny had a stack of old magazines in her attic. She never threw away a thing. Said it might come in handy some day. I used to spend hours looking at them books. 'Course, the dresses didn't suit my style. I got a style all my own, you might say. But I thought they had a sort of flair, so I decided if I ever had me one of them bow-tiks this is the kind of thing I'd sell. Do you think anybody'd buy them?"

"Yes," Jessie said. She looked up and saw Blake's smile in the rearview mirror. She smiled back. "Yes, Wanda Lou. I certainly do."

Eight

Jessie became caught up in the high-flying dreams of Wanda Lou as the flamboyant hitchhiker pulled another stunning creation from her duffle bag.

"I'm simply amazed, Wanda Lou," she said. "Where did you get the material for these dresses?"

"Garage sales, mostly. It's a sight what folks will sell for a dollar. Evening gowns that must 'a cost a small fortune to begin with. I'd take off the spangles and such, rip 'em up, and start all over."

"Do you have a portfolio of designs?"

"A port-what?"

For a moment, Jessie had forgotten that she wasn't dealing with a professional. "I'm sorry. Do you have drawings of your dresses?"

"Just in my head."

"And you make all of these yourself?"

"Just me and my needle. I got quite a talent, don't I?" She smiled proudly.

"Indeed, you do."

"When I get to New Orleans, I'm gonna make me some money and then I'm gonna open the finest bow-tik this side of the Miss'sippi. I might even be able to afford one of them little ole 'lectric sewing machines where you just push the pedal and it does all the work. Why, I might just . . ."

Wanda Lou talked on and on, spinning her dreams, while Jessie studied the dresses. They were superbly designed and well constructed. With the right supervision and the right backing, Wanda Lou could become the next Chloe.

With a suddenness that often characterized her decisions, Jessie leaned forward and spoke to Blake.

"Stop the bus."

"Now?" he asked.

"As soon as we get to the next phone, stop the bus."

"Are you thinking what I think you're thinking?"

Jessie laughed. "What kind of a question is that for a university professor? And the answer is yes."

"You're remarkable, Jessie."

"Thank you, Blake. At times you're pretty wonderful too."

Wanda Lou hadn't paid the slightest bit of attention to their conversation. She was still spinning her dreams.

". . . and I thought I'd call myself Monique. It's a good foreign-soundin' name. Kinda mysterious and sexy. Besides that, who'd want to buy clothes from a girl named Wanda Lou?"

Jessie turned to her. "I do."

Wanda Lou's mouth fell open. "You do? I mean you really and truly sure fire as hell do? You're not just puttin' me on? I mean, you actually want to buy my little ole dresses?" She patted her hands over her ears. "My ears must need cleanin' out." She leaned forward and shouted near Blake's ear. "Did she say that to me or am I just dreamin'?"

After his ears stopped ringing, Blake smiled. "She said it. Jessie owns a chain of department stores, Wanda Lou."

"Well, hot damn!"

"Wanda Lou," Jessie said, "I'd like to sell your dresses—on a trial basis, of course—in my department stores."

"Whoopee!"

"There are a lot of details to be worked out, but I have a friend who can take care of that."

Blake glanced at her in the mirror. "Hunter?"

"Hunter. He's always wanted to be a Pygmalion."

Wanda Lou cast Jessie a dubious look. "I'm not sure I want to be hooked up with a pig hunter. What kind of friend is that anyhow? Somebody who goes around chasing innocent little pigs?"

Jessie bit her lip to keep from laughing. "He doesn't chase pigs. His name is Hunter, Hunter Chadwick. You'll love him."

And Wanda Lou did.

Jessie called Hunter from Woodville and he met them at the airport in Baton Rouge that evening.

He didn't even blink as his lively black eyes surveyed the outrageous Wanda Lou. "My dear, we are going to get along famously." He bent over her hand and kissed it, winning Wanda Lou's heart forever.

"Well, hot damn. Looks like this pig hunter's turned out to be a prince."

"That's exactly what he is, Wanda Lou," Jessie said, smiling fondly at her old friend. "He's a prince of a guy. Are you sure this is what you want to do? I don't mean to rush you into making a decision you'll regret. It's not too late to change your mind about signing with Wentworths. Blake can take you on to New Orleans."

Wanda Lou propped her hands on her outthrust hips. "I been dreamin' and dreamin' about what I'd do if I ever got to New Orleans, but it might turn out to be just that. A dream. Dreams're nice, but they don't feed you and they don't keep you warm at night." She glanced from Jessie to Hunter. "Anyhow, seems like I been dreamin' about black-eyed peas when I could 'a been dreamin' about ham and gravy."

Hunter's laugh was uninhibited and hearty. "I've never been called ham and gravy before. I like it." He took Wanda Lou's elbow. "Our chariot awaits, Wanda Lou."

"That's Monique," she said. "I left Wanda Lou behind in Natchez. I'm startin' my new life as Monique."

Blake and Jessie watched them board the plane.

"That was a generous thing you did, Jessie."

"It was business."

"Even so, it takes generosity to risk so much on a woman you hardly know."

She smiled up at him. "I have an instinct about these things."

"Learning to go with your feelings, Jessie?"

"Only in business matters, friend."

He didn't miss the slight emphasis she put on the last word. He tried to cover his disappointment with a smile, but it showed in his eyes. He wanted things to be different. He wanted to take her in his arms and kiss her until she was breathless. He wanted to run his hands through that black satin hair and cradle her head on his shoulder. He wanted to wave a magic wand and banish Rick from her mind forever. Instead, he took her hand and led her back to the bus.

Sandy barked a welcome from her basket, and even the doves cooed at having them back. Jessie started toward her curtained-off cubicle.

"Jessie. Wait." His voice was urgent.

She turned. The naked desire in his eyes made her grip the back of the seat. She stood very still, waiting for him to speak.

"Don't keep denying us," he said.

"I'm not . . ." She stopped. There was no use lying. She was denying them. She was shutting down her feelings because of things that had nothing to do with Blake. "You're right. I am."

"I'm not like Rick and Harry. I'm not an invention of your mind. I'm real, Jessie. I know who I am and what I want. And I want you."

"Don't you think I know that? Every time I see that look in your eyes, I melt inside. Lying behind that curtain at night—knowing you want me, wanting you—is sheer torture."

"Then what's stopping you, Jessie?"

"Don't push, Blake. You promised to be my friend."

"I am your friend. Friends help each other to see the truth. And the truth is you're giving the past an importance it doesn't deserve. People should learn from their mistakes and move forward."

"That's easy for you to say. You're a psychologist."

"I'm a man, too, Jessie."

She gripped the seat so hard her knuckles turned white. He needn't have pointed out the obvious, she thought. He was a man, a special man, an extraordinary man, all bronzed muscle and golden hair and silver eyes. He had depth and tenderness and strength. He had humor and compassion and courage. But he was also human and therefore fallible.

"What if I'm wrong?" she asked. "What if I go with my feelings and then discover I've made another mistake? I don't think I can stand that—to make another mistake." She raked a shaky hand through her hair. "You're right: you are a man. And I'm a woman. We're people, Blake. People mistakes can't be written off as tax losses."

"Dammit, Jessie." He looked at the stubborn thrust of her chin, the green challenge in her eyes. There didn't seem to be anything more to say. He had thought the past was behind her after she had told him about Rick, but apparently he had been wrong. The scars were too deep. She still needed time. And time was running out.

He crossed the space between them and took her into his arms. Rubbing his hands across her rigid back, he leaned down and murmured, "Friends, Jessie. If that's the way it has to be—just good friends."

He caressed her until she relaxed against him. Then he tilted her chin up with an index finger.

"What would it take to bring that beautiful smile out of hiding?"

"Magic."

"Then you shall have it." Releasing her, he bowed gallantly. "A special show just for you."

He led her to the passenger seat, and Sandy hopped into her lap. With a flourish, he donned his cape and top hat.

He produced roses, a dozen magic yellow roses that floated out of the top hat and swirled around the table. She was enchanted. He made the doves disappear and reappear in unusual places until the whole bus seemed to be humming with their song. She was bewitched. Silk scarves in all the colors of the rainbow danced over his shoulders. She was enthralled.

She clapped her hands with the uninhibited delight of a child. Her eyes sparkled and her mouth turned up at the corners. And she forgot. She forgot Rick's long-ago betrayal. She forgot the brief humiliation of Harry. She even forgot Wentworth Enterprises and the vast wealth that isolated her. She forgot everything except the man and his magic. And when he made a monarch butterfly float through the air and hover near her lips, she felt as if she had been branded. Blake had woven a spell around her and set his seal upon her. And she was forever his.

They found a lovely park and stayed in Baton Rouge three days. Blake performed magic shows and counseled a whole string of people who flocked to him like bees to honey. Jessie, watching everything from her self-imposed distance, knew that she was falling in love. She knew that he was no ordinary man. There was a joy and a generosity in his spirit that lifted her up. Watching him work his healing magic on the people who came to him filled her with pride.

She wanted to do something special for him, to show him how much the trip meant to her, to show how much she cared. And so she started a secret project. Perhaps inspired by the exalted visions of Wanda Lou, Jessie purchased yarn and needles and instruction books and started knitting Blake a sweater. At night while he sat at the table working on his research notes, she sat behind the curtain clicking her needles.

He pretended not to know what was going on. Sometimes he would drag a red herring across her path by asking, "What are you doing back there, Jessie?"

"Doing my nails," she'd sometimes reply or, "Just reading."

He would smile and go back to his work. Day by day he fell more and more in love with Jessie. He watched her gallantly cover her distaste at doing dishes and valiantly conquer her habits of untidiness. He saw the great effort she made to live in a simplified world with canned beans and a folding cot. She handled the hobo life-style with grace and charm, and he knew that they had bridged the gap between their separate worlds. Her great wealth and his relative poverty didn't matter anymore. What mattered was who they were inside.

Except for the ghost of Rick, they might have come together. They might have torn down the curtain that separated them and completed the journey as lovers. They might have made the bus live up to its name.

But the ghost of her past was still there, and Blake respected that. After the talk in Baton Rouge, he made a conscious effort to back off and give Jessie the time she needed. He was her friend, her confidant. The hugs he gave her were nonthreatening. In every way, he tried to make her life simple and joyful. He hoped that an interlude of ordinariness would help her put the past in perspective.

It was raining when they left Baton Rouge. The water came down in icy gray sheets that swathed the bus and obscured the road. It beat against the windows and hammered on the roof. Its insistent rhythm seemed to permeate the bus.

Jessie shivered. Blake saw the movement in the rearview mirror.

"Are you cold?" he asked.

"No. I don't like rain."

"Why?"

She peered through the thick curtain of rain at the dreary bogs of Louisiana. "I think it must have rained every day after I married Rick. I'd never been so cold or so miserable in all my life. The old apartment was damp and clammy. I missed Mississippi—the warm Indian summers, the slow pace of the days. It rained and rained. I felt as if my skin were covered with cold mist. And I wanted . . ." Her voice trailed off, and she was lost in remembering. She had wanted more than pretty words; she had wanted to be touched. She had wanted more than poetry; she had wanted sex.

Watching her in the mirror, seeing the pain that crowded in behind the memories, Blake silently cursed the boy who had caused it all.

"It's just rain, Jessie."

"I guess it's symbolic."

"Some people call it a blessing. It makes things grow. It cleanses and refreshes."

She smiled. "That's lovely. Are you a poet?"

He grimaced. "Hell, no. Not even remotely."

"What a relief."

She turned her face again to the window, and Blake drove the bus in silence. The only sounds were the pounding of raindrops and the drumming of Jessie's fingernails. Baton Rouge was far behind, and one little parish town blurred into the next.

Suddenly Blake spoke. "I have an idea. Would you like to drive, Jessie?"

"That's not an idea; that's an inspiration." She laughed. "Of course I'd like to drive."

"I thought so." Leaning forward, he tried to see ahead, to find a place to pull over. "I remember how you love to whip that Ferrari of yours around."

"Driving will give me something to do. Magic shows are fine, and meeting people does help pass the time of day, but I'm accustomed to activity." She pointed. "Look, Blake. Up ahead. Pull over."

He eased the bus to a stop at a small roadside rest area. "You're so excited. I don't know why I didn't think of this sooner."

They exchanged places and she eagerly scanned the dashboard.

"Do you think you can handle it?" he asked. Now that he'd had the idea, Blake was having second thoughts. Driving a bus wasn't as easy as driving a car, and the bus was old and somewhat crotchety, and what if she had a wreck? He'd never forgive himself. He sat forward in his seat. "Jessie—"

"Don't even think about changing your mind, Dr. Blake Montgomery. I can drive anything on wheels." Putting the bus back into gear, she steered exuberantly out into the rain.

"This is great," she said. A parish town whizzed by as she gunned the old bus down the road.

Blake held onto the edges of his seat and tried to look comfortable. "This reminds me of going to camp when I was a child. We used to bounce around on our seats and sing silly songs."

"You're too big to bounce and your singing is terrible."

He gave a mock-injured look. "Madame, I resemble that remark."

She laughed. "You certainly do."

"Just for that, I'll have to sing my specialty." He started a loud off-key rendition of "Ninety-nine Bottles of Beer on the Wall."

By the time he had gotten to ninety-seven, Jessie joined him. The old bus zipped merrily along, filled with laughter and silly song. About thirty miles out of New Orleans, the rains slackened and became a mist. Although he would have preferred traveling at a much more sedate pace, Blake was beginning to relax.

Right in the middle of thirty-nine bottles of beer, Jessie stopped singing. "Good grief! A turtle!" The old bus rocked as she swerved out of the turtle's path. If it hadn't been raining, she might have made it, but the road was slick and the bus was big. There was a mighty grinding sound as The Joy Bus plowed into a ditch.

Blake was instantly out of his seat, fighting to keep his balance. "Jessie! Are you all right?"

Still holding the steering wheel in a death grip, she turned a stricken face to him. "I think I skinned my knee and I broke a fingernail and—"

He hugged her so close it hurt her ribs. "Thank God, you're all right."

"I wrecked your bus," she wailed against his shoulder.

"Shh." He patted her back. "We're just in a ditch."

"I don't want to be in a ditch."

He rubbed his face against her hair. "It's okay. We'll be out before you know it."

She pulled back and looked up at him. "Are you sure, Blake?"

"Trust me, Jessie."

"I do."

"If you're all right now, I'll hop out and see what needs to be done."

"I'm going too."

"No. You stay here. It's cold outside."

"Dammit, Blake. I got the bus in the ditch and I'll help get it out."

"I guess there's no use arguing."

"None whatsoever."

Together they surveyed the damage. The right fender was crumpled and one headlight was crushed where the bus had rammed into the wet embankment. The front tires were mired up to the axle in mud.

"If I can find enough branches and place them under the wheels, maybe we can ease out," Blake said.

He crossed the ditch and began to pull branches off a pine tree. Jessie tromped after him, her fur coat dragging in the tall wet grass and her boots sinking up to the heels in the black mud.

"I suppose there are snakes here as big as my leg," she said.

"Probably. But look on the bright side. They'll be too cold to bite."

"That's a bright side?"

Within fifteen minutes Blake declared they had enough branches under the bus wheels. Jessie huddled on the passenger seat, chilled and disgruntled, as he put the bus into gear. The wheels spun uselessly in the mire. He tried again without success.

"We'll be here forever," Jessie said glumly.

"If I have to be somewhere forever, I'm glad you're with me."

"How can you be so damned cheerful?" She got up and looked out the window on the opposite side of the bus. "Where are we, anyway?"

"I didn't notice a sign," he said over the revving of the engine. "I was too busy singing."

"This place probably doesn't even have a name. Who'd want to name the backside of nowhere?" She sat back down and propped her chin on her hands. "I don't want to ever hear that song again."

He turned to her. "I think we're going to need help getting out. I noticed a store about half a mile down the road. I'll walk back and phone for help."

"I don't know whether to go with you and freeze to death or stay here and let the snakes and the Cajans get me."

He laughed. "Cheer up, Jessie. This will all be fun when you get it in perspective."

"I'm not holding my breath." Although the inside of the bus was warm, she pulled her coat up around her neck and scrunched into a corner. "Go on. I want to be miserable all by myself."

Leaning down, he kissed her cheek. "I'll be right back, Jessie."

He was gone thirty minutes, the longest thirty minutes of Jessie's life. She jumped at every sound. She imagined that he had been hit by a passing truck and was lying on the roadside, bloody and suffering. She thought she heard people trying to get into the back of the bus. She saw movement out the window and decided it was an alligator.

Sandy jumped into her lap, more to be comforted than to comfort.

"Dammit, Sandy. I'm not used to this kind of adversity. If this is the good life, I hate it."

She thought how much simpler life had been in Jackson, where all she had to do was pick up the car phone and call for help. She thought how nice it would be to sink into a huge tub with bubbles up to her neck and to know the maid was in the next room laying out her clothes. She thought how good lobster dripping with butter would taste.

"I hate 'Ninety-nine bottles of beer on the wall'," she said fiercely. Then she thought about Blake and she was sorry she'd said it. She thought about the way he smiled, the way his eyes sparkled when he looked at her, the way his voice sounded when he sang, off-key and comic, yet oddly comforting.

"What am I going to do, Sandy? I love that man."

By the time Blake returned, Jessie had worked herself into a state close to tears. He arrived in a stalwart wrecker with a dour little man whose sole comment was, "Leave it to Louey."

"What does that mean?" Jessie asked Blake as Louey walked around the bus scowling. "Is he going to get us out of this ditch?"

"I have confidence in him," Blake said. That was stretching the truth a bit, he decided, but it was worth it to see Jessie smile again. "Sit tight. I'm going back outside to discuss this situation with Louey."

"From what I've seen of Louey, I think you'd have better luck discussing the situation with the alligators."

"What alligators?"

"The ones waiting out there to bite your legs off."

"I'm glad to see your sense of humor is back."

"Don't count on it."

She pressed her face to the window. What she saw did nothing to improve her mood. Blake, as usual, looked calm and untroubled, but Louey gestured wildly and even tore his steel wool hair.

"I think it's going to be a bad day at Black Rock, Sandy," she told the small dog.

Blake returned to the bus, still looking cheerful. "The bus has a broken axle, which will take a few days to repair. Louey is going to drive us to a motel for the duration. We'll take a few clothes and the animals, of course." He started to pack.

"I'm sorry about ths bus," she said, "but I can't say I'm sorry about the motel." She stood up, dumping Sandy off her lap. "Just think. A big tub and plenty of hot water and a real bed. It will be sheer luxury."

Jessie's hopes were short-lived. They piled into Louey's stalwart wrecker with a few belongings and Blake's animals and bounced along in silence to the motel.

"This is *it*?" Jessie wailed when Louey pulled into a small parking lot. A garish neon sign with one *p* missing proclaimed the motel to be The Bluebird of Happiness. Four lopsided units looked as if they had last been whitewashed during the fifties. Dried weeds, higher than Jessie's knees, were clumped around the sagging doors.

She turned a stricken face to Blake. "Can't we go somewhere else?"

"This is it, lady," Louey said, "the only motel in town." His grin showed his gold-capped teeth. It was the first time they had seen him smile. "Damn fine motel. No bugs." He parked the wrecker, swung down, and started unloading their bags. "My cousin Charlie, damn fine man, first cousin twice remove, on my mama's side. He own the motel."

Jessie wished he would shut up. She hated his habit of dropping the endings of words. "Leave it to Louey, indeed," she muttered as Blake helped her down from the cab. Then, feeling guilty that she was making a bad situation worse, she smiled bravely. "At least we'll both have beds," she said.

Louey's cousin Charlie beamed at his customers, patted them on the back with weather-reddened hands, and immediately dashed Jessie's hopes. "Bug man come to spray today. Hose busted up right bad 'fore he finished. You lucky. Got one unit left. No fumes, plenty hot water, no rats." He took a key from the pegboard behind his desk. "Yessir, this your lucky day."

Jessie thought she might cry. She thought she might embarrass herself by bursting into tears right there in the middle of that wretched motel office.

"Blake." It was a small plea.

"We need separate rooms," Blake told Charlie. "Is there any way we can use two units?"

"No way, buddy, 'less you want to suffocate like the bugs. Too much bug spray. Rooms have to be aired 'fore they can be used." He tossed a key to Blake. "Follow me."

I won't cry, Jessie told herself as she followed them to the room. The mist dampened her hair and the mud clumped onto her boots. *I'll be a trooper. I got us into this mess, the least I can do is act decent about it.* Her pep talk held back the tears until Charlie stowed their two bags, the rabbits, Sandy, and the doves into a tiny room that was barely big enough for one.

"We can make do," Blake said. Even his good cheer made her want to cry. "I can put the animal baskets in the closet to make more room. We'll leave the door open." As he talked he began putting their belongings in order. "I'm accustomed to small spaces." He glanced toward the sagging bed. "You can take the bed and I'll sleep on the floor."

She made a strangled sound and he turned quickly toward her.

"Jessie?"

She plunged through the bathroom door before he could see her face. "I'm going to take a bath," she called through the closed door.

"That sounds like a good idea."

She locked the door, turned the faucets on full blast, and began stripping off her clothes. She tried to concentrate on undressing. She tried telling herself that this, too, would pass. She tried telling herself that she was being childish, that she making mountains out of molehills. Nothing worked.

By the time she was in the water, tears were streaming down her cheeks. She grimaced at the dingy washcloth, then plunged it into the water and vigorously scrubbed her face. The harder she tried to choke back her tears, the faster they came. She buried her face in the washcloth and sobbed.

Blake heard the sound and stiffened. "Jessie," he called.

The sound of his voice made her cry even harder.

He dropped the dove cages and crossed to the bathroom door. "Are you all right in there?"

Her only response was an increase in decibels of her wailing.

He rattled the doorknob. "Let me in, Jessie."

She cried even louder.

Panic seized him. "I'm coming in, Jessie." He tackled the door with his shoulder and burst into the bathroom. Jessie was huddled in the tub, crying into her washcloth.

Without thought, he scooped her out of the water and held her, dripping, against his chest. "What's wrong, Jessie? Are you hurt?" He crushed her to him and murmured into her hair. "Speak to me, love. What's the matter?"

"Oh, Bla-ake." She clung to him, rubbing her face against his neck. "He said . . . it had . . . no rats." She spoke brokenly through her sobs.

"Is that all, love? I thought you'd been hurt in the wreck more seriously than you told me." He smiled into her hair. "Of course it has no rats. It's too cold for rats."

"And bugs . . . snakes . . . and alligators. I ha-hate Louis-iana."

He cuddled her close. "No, you don't, love. It's just a reaction."

She shook her head and sobbed into his shirt collar. "I'm sick . . . of canned soup . . . and folding cots . . . and dirty dishes. I want . . . I want . . ." She couldn't go on for her crying. She pressed closer to him, clinging to him.

He rubbed his face against her hair, murmured soothing words into her ear. "It's all right, love. Go ahead and get it out of your system. There now. I'm here, sweet Jessie."

Gradually her sobs turned to sniffles and her sniffles to sighs. She heaved a great breath and relaxed against his chest.

He smiled down at her. "That's better, Jessie."

She tilted her head back and looked into his face. Suddenly she felt the muscles in his arms tense, saw the flame quicken in his eyes. And she was aware of her nakedness.

"Jessie?" The word was a whisper, a plea, a promise.

And she surrendered. Her arms tightened around him.

"Yes, Blake. Oh, yes," she said before his lips descended on hers.

Nine

Blake placed her tenderly on the bed and stood looking down at her. In the dim flash of the neon motel sign, her skin had the luster of satin and the coloring of warm honey. He knelt beside the bed and traced her body with one finger. He traced the exotic slant of her eyes, the high cheekbones, her determined chin, the delicate line of her throat. His forefinger drew a small circle over her thrumming pulse, then journeyed downward to arouse her dusky rose nipples.

"You're beautiful, Jessie." His voice was filled with wonder. "Almost too beautiful to touch."

"Touch me, Blake," she whispered. "I want to be touched by you."

He stripped off his clothes and lay down beside her. With one hand on her back, he turned her until they were facing each other, bodies not touching but so close that she could feel the warmth of him, like a soft desert wind. His breath stirred the black satin hair upon her cheek.

"I love you, Jessie. I've loved you from the moment you stepped out of that red Ferrari."

"And I love you, Blake. I think from the moment I saw your hair, I was lost." She reached out and ran her hand lovingly through the bright locks that had fallen across his forehead. "Your hair is beautiful. I love it."

He put his hand on the curve of her hip and traced the top of her thigh, then dipped downward to cup the thick curls at the base of her flat stomach. "So perfect," he whispered. "I feel as if I'm lying with a mythological creature, a goddess."

"I'm real, Blake." Her fingers twined in his thick golden hair, and she drew his head tenderly toward her breast. "I'm real. Taste me."

And he did. Pleasure exploded within her as his mouth and tongue discovered her shape, texture, and taste. Her fingers tightened in his hair, pulling him closer.

"Oh, yes, Blake. Like that." She felt as if her entire life had been a prelude to this moment. Arching her back, she offered the full ripeness of her breasts, and he took them. Deliciously. Gloriously. Fully. His hands kneaded. His tongue teased. His mouth suckled.

"I can't get enough of you, Jessie," he murmured. His muscles were bunched, tense with anticipation. He was rigid, ready to explode. But he held himself in check. He wanted to prolong the pleasure. He wanted to savor her, to make everything perfect for her.

She moaned with protest as he lifted himself on his elbows to look down at her. His hand touched her taut nipples, moved down the flat planes of her stomach, caressed her silky mound. "This is mine, Jessie." His voice was thick with desire. "So beautiful and all mine."

"Yes, Blake." She arched against his exploring hand. "Please." It was a whispered cry, an urgent plea for fulfillment.

And he answered. Bending down, he scored her stomach with his tongue, circled her mound, and nibbled the inner softness of her thighs.

She felt as if all the heat in the world had settled between her thighs. His fingers parted her. She pushed herself against his questing tongue. Colored lights exploded inside her head, and she had the feeling of entering a rainbow.

She sighed.

He explored.

And when the sweet ecstasy became too much to bear, he lifted her hips. She arched. He plunged. They ignited. Heightened by the waiting, their passion became an almost visible cloak of fire that wrapped around them, glowing, searing, burning, and finally consuming. It was wonder. It was magic. It was love.

The cheap motel room, lit by the gaudy neon sign, was transformed into a romantic pleasure palace. The sagging bed with rusty, squeaking springs might have been covered with satin sheets for all the lovers knew. The water-stained wallpaper and the cracked lamp could have been the finest decor in the Waldorf for all they cared. Dr. Blake Montgomery was loving his Jessie Wentworth, and nothing mattered except the two of them and the skyrocketing feelings they were exchanging.

And after the final fulfillment came, they lay, covers entangled, bodies entwined in the flashing blue light of The Bluebird of Happiness.

Blake gently touched the blue *H* on Jessie's hip. "It's prophetic, I think."

Her tongue flicked over the wavy neon *B* on

his chest. "I hope so." Suddenly she closed her arms around him and squeezed so hard his breath whooshed out. "Hold me, Blake."

He pulled her fiercely to him. "Always, my beautiful Jessie."

"Don't ever let go," she murmured into his golden mat of chest hair.

"I won't."

"You promise?"

Her plea drove nails through his heart, and he knew she was seeing ghosts. "I promise." He kissed her hair, her forehead, her ear, her eyelids. "I'm here, Jessie, loving you. We'll make it. Together, we'll make it."

She tilted her head back and looked into his eyes. They were sincere and honest and filled with such love, her heart turned over. Suddenly she knew they would make it. They had bridged their separate worlds and forged a bond that couldn't be broken. They had held their passion at bay and built a relationship on mutual respect and trust.

She rested her head in the valley over his heart and sighed, letting go the past, releasing her ghosts. His heart gladdened as he felt her relax.

"I'm free," she said.

"I'm glad."

They held each other while the shadows deepened in the room, until the only light was a faint blue glow from the flashing motel sign. And their passion quickened again.

This time there was an exuberance to their joining, a joy that flowed between them, lifting them until they were floating high in that special realm that only true lovers can know. The second time around their coming together was yellow roses and candlelight, river song and moonlight. It was giving and receiving and filling and easing. It was love.

Afterward, the room was quiet except for the soft sighs of their sleep and the cooing of doves.

Jessie woke up to the sound of Blake's off-key singing. She smiled and yawned and stretched and thought that she'd never been in a more wonderful place than The Bluebird of Happiness. After bounding out of bed, she tapped on the bathroom door.

"Who is it?" Blake called.

"Who are you rexpecting?"

"The sexiest back scrubber in Louisiana."

"I'm sexy but I don't scrub backs."

"You'll do. Come on in."

She pushed open the door. The impact of seeing Blake sitting in the tub hit her right in the pit of her stomach. The golden hair on his chest sparkled with water, and his freshly washed honey and wheat hair looked like a crown.

"Excuse me," she said. "I must be in the wrong century. You look like a Greek god."

He grinned and held out his hand. "Come here." He made room between his legs, and she joined him in the tub.

Leaning her back against his wet chest, she smiled over her shoulder at him. "I've always wanted to share a bath with somebody."

He scooped a handful of water and dribbled it across her breasts. "Name your fantasies, Beautiful Lady, and I'll make them all come true."

"With hocus pocus?"

"No. Magic." He took the soap and lathered her, slowly, sensuously.

A wonderful heat spread throughout her body.

"If I could bottle this feeling and sell it, I'd be rich."

"You already are."

Pressing back onto the bulging evidence of his desire, she became a vessel, waiting to be filled.

"Do you want to know another of my fantasies?" Her question was breathless.

"I think it's the same as mine." He turned her around, lifting and fitting her until they were one.

There was no more talk as they made their fantasy come true.

Afterward Blake borrowed Charlie's car, a vintage Buick, and went to get food. The rains had started again, but this time Jessie wasn't bothered. She felt cozy and protected and loved.

While Blake was gone she worked on her secret knitting project. The sleeves didn't seem to be shaping up exactly right, but she wasn't daunted. Blake would think the sweater wonderful no matter what it looked like.

The rain continued for three days, and The Bluebird of Happiness Motel became their private hideaway. The joy they took in each other was endless. Had it not been for Charlie, they would never have left the room except for food.

On the third morning they awakened to a loud battering on their door. Blake yanked on his pants and called, "Coming."

"It's just me. Charlie."

"I'll be out in a minute, Charlie."

He finished dressing, kissed Jessie's love-pouted mouth, and left the room. When he returned, he was laughing.

"I'll need a magician's assistant, Jessie. This is a command performance."

"Who?" Jessie climbed reluctantly out of her warm bed and began to dress.

"Charlie's relatives. He and Louey have spread the word that a magician is in town, and the relatives have gathered for a show."

She fastened her green wool slacks and pulled on a matching cable-knit sweater. "Let's run up to the office and do a quick show. I'm selfish. I want you all to myself."

"His relatives won't fit in the office, Jessie. They're gathered in the community center."

"How many does he have? Sixteen?"

"I think I'll let you be surprised."

They banged and rattled across town in the backseat of Charlie's old Buick. Sandy kept watch over the doves and the rabbits in the front seat.

"Yessir," Charlie said as he drove, "I guess the last time we had a magic show was when Houdini come to town. Back in the early twenties. 'Course nobody remembers it 'cept Aunt Eller, and she don't always tell it right." He swiveled around to look at Blake, and the old car swayed perilously close to a ditch. "You got all them handcuffs and things? Escape. That's what Aunt Eller likes. It don't do to displease Aunt Eller."

"Do you think they'll lynch us if we displease this old matriarch, Blake?" Jessie whispered.

"If we die, we'll die together," he said with mock solemnity.

The community center was packed with Charlie's kin.

"There must be a hundred people here," Jessie said.

"Hundred fifteen," Charlie said proudly. " 'Course lots of 'em's twice removed, but they count just the same. Kin is kin, no matter how thin the blood. Look'a yonder. There's Aunt Eller." His voice was filled with pride. "Still spry as a goose and twice as mean."

A tiny shriveled-up woman with a face as lined as a river map held court in the center of the room. She was seated in an oak rocker and surrounded by squirming children. Her black dress with a yellowed lace collar looked as though it had come from somebody's attic.

Pointing a palsied finger at Blake, she asked in a quavering voice, "Is that the magic feller?"

"Yes, ma'am, Aunt Eller," Charlie said.

"Start the show. I been waitin' sixty years to see if Houdini got outa that trunk."

"That's not Houdini, Granny," a teenage girl said.

"No use tellin' her, Lilly Mae," Charlie said. "Once she sets her mind, there's no changin' it."

"I don't like this, Blake," Jessie said.

He put his arm around her. "It'll be all right, Jessie. It's all a part of my research. Do you see those careworn faces over there?" He nodded in the direction of a group of middle-aged men and women. "If a small interlude of magic can take them away from the harsh realities of life and bring them joy, then this trip is worthwhile."

She smiled at him. As always, Blake put everything in perspective and made her feel secure.

"You expect to find another grateful person?" she asked.

"Certainly. The bet's still on and I intend to win. I can't wait to get you alone in my humble professor's cottage."

The look in his eyes held promises that took her breath away. She wanted desperately for him to win the bet, she realized. She wanted him to be right about the correlation between innocence and joy. Hadn't he already given her so much joy that it fairly spilled over? She wanted to go with him to the university. She wanted to stay in his cottage. She knew him as a man of magic. She wanted to know him also as a psychology professor.

"Then let's get on with the show," she said.

Blake, with Jessie's assistance, performed his show under the baleful eye of Aunt Eller. When it was over she rapped her cane on the floor and complained about not seeing a trunk wrapped in chains. But the rest of the relatives were overjoyed. The smiles on their faces reflected their happiness. Only one of them, however, came forward.

Taking Blake's hand, Arthur Landeux, Charlie's uncle, expressed his gratitude. "Young man, you've made me forget the mortgage on my farm. You've made me forget last year's bad crop and the tractor that's not paid for, For a little while, I was a kid again."

"Magic seems to do that," Blake said.

"I guess as long as there's some magic and some laughter in this world, there's hope," Arthur said.

"There's always hope."

After Arthur left, Jessie turned to Blake. "That makes four."

He grinned. "Are you counting?"

"It's my bet too."

Charlie helped them load the animals back into the Buick. As he backed out of the parking lot, he told Blake, "Louey said your bus is ready. Want me to take you by to get it?"

Blake reached for Jessie's hand and squeezed it. The touch communicated his feelings. It said, I don't want this to end.

"Take me by the motel first," Jessie said to

Charlie. Looking into Blake's eyes, she whispered, "There's something I have to do."

He traced her lips with one finger. "Wait for me there, Jessie."

The Joy Bus looked like a proud old lady with too much rouge on her cheeks. Louey had hammered out the bent fender and applied a new coat of paint to cover the marks. The new paint was a shade brighter than the original pink, so he had painted the other fender to match. Blake thought his old bus now had a rakish look that entirely suited his mood. He was feeling rather rakish himself. The sun had finally broken through the clouds, and the woman of his dreams was waiting for him at the motel.

He thanked Louey effusively, paid him too much, hurried into his bus, and roared down the road at an unaccustomed breakneck speed. His heart throbbed a fierce rhythm as he parked his bus under The Bluebird of Happiness sign.

Jessie was waiting for him. He opened the door and there she was, lying in the middle of the bed, the Russian sable coat spread beneath her, hair fanned out like a bolt of black silk, skin luminescent in the rays of sunshine that slanted through the window. He caught his breath at her naked splendor.

She lifted one graceful arm. "Come. One more fantasy, my darling."

"I like this fantasy." His clothes drifted to the floor as he advanced toward the bed. "Very much."

The bedsprings squeaked under his weight.

"Lie on your back, Blake."

The sable caressed his back, sleek and sensuous. Jessie leaned over him, spreading her hair across his chest. He lifted the silky strands to his lips and inhaled their fragrance. His senses reeled with the nearness of Jessie. He felt as if he were drowning in luxury.

Her tongue touched him, pink, catlike, delicate. She traced his cheekbones, his chin, his mouth. He tingled. She slid down his body, searing his throat, his nipples, his navel with her tongue. He ached. She moved lower, her mouth closing around him. He exploded.

"Jessie, Jessie," he murmured as sensations rocked his body. He was aware of satin flesh, silky hair, sleek sable. His toes curled under. Warmth, fragrance, sunlight, neon, flames. He went wild.

And Jessie was with him, all the way. Every touch, every sensation, every movement was like a symphony. The sable coat became damp. The sun's rays slanted lower across the floor. And still they spent their love, freely, exuberantly.

Finally, release.

Afterward she lay in the curve of his arm. He brushed her damp hair back from her forehead.

"I love you, Jessie."

"I'll never let you forget that, Blake."

The Bluebird of Happiness was a lovely memory, and New Orleans was spread before them like a bawdy woman, raucous and flamboyant and pulsing with life.

As they drove into the city Jessie leaned forward eagerly. "This city is made for lovers, Blake. Let's park the bus and check into the Roosevelt. Let's walk down Bourbon Street and eat shrimp po' boys and listen to jazz. My treat."

In the rearview mirror he saw the sparkle of her

eyes, the roses in her cheeks. He could no more deny her than he could sprout wings and fly.

"What about the animals?" he asked.

"I know the manager. We'll rent a separate room for them, hire an animal sitter."

"That's extravagant."

"That's love." She hugged herself. "I'm in love, Blake. For the first time in my life, I'm in love. Indulge me."

And so the strange group checked into two rooms at the Roosevelt. Jessie paid a small fortune for an animal sitter, and she and Blake went out on the town. The city embraced them. It enticed them. It cajoled them. It entertained them. When they were sated with bright lights and good food and jazz music, they walked beside the river, coats pulled high around their ears, holding each other for warmth.

Arm in arm, they listened to the Mississippi sing its familiar song, and they were content. The chill from the night wind finally drove them inside. They took a horse-drawn buggy back to their hotel, laughed their way through the lobby, and squeezed each other tight all the way up to their room.

They loved until the dawn pinked the window-sill. Then they fell asleep, thinking that nothing could drive them apart.

Jesssie watched the magic show from the back of the auditorium. This was Blake's last chance to win the bet. Tomorrow they would leave New Orleans and head back to Jackson. She looked from Blake to the faces of the people in the audience. Not one single person appeared to be the grateful kind. For a moment, she felt defeated, then a plan began to form in her mind.

She hurried out to the bus to get her sable coat. When she returned she moved around the back of the chilly room, hoping to spot a likely candidate. She saw one woman sitting off to the side, her faded dress and wrinkled stockings showing beneath a patched coat.

Jessie sat down beside her. "May I sit here?"

The woman smiled at her. "Certainly."

The woman, Lorene Dempling, exhibited an open friendliness that made Jessie's plan feasible. By the time the magic show was over, she had struck a deal with the woman that would assure Blake's success in winning the bet.

"Remember," Jessie cautioned as Mrs. Dempling rose to express her gratitude to Blake, "he must not know about my part in this."

"I'll remember," the woman said. "And I'll never forget what you've done for me." She pulled Jessie's fur coat over her tattered clothes and moved forward.

Jessie watched from the back of the auditorium as Mrs. Dampling approached Blake. She saw his smile of pleasure. She watched Mrs. Dempling say her rehearsed speech. At least, she assumed it was the rehearsed speech. They were too far away for her to hear their conversation. And then the unexpected happened. Mrs. Dempling swung her arms wide, revealing the faded, patched clothes beneath the Russian sable. Jessie saw Blake's face change, saw him lean forward to look closely at the coat, saw him say something to Mrs. Dempling. The woman became flustered, shook her head in denial, and hurried away.

Blake scanned the auditorium until he saw Jessie. Even across the vast space that separated them, she could feel the tension in him. She thrust her chin out and returned his look. She had done nothing wrong, she reasoned. She had merely done a good deed and in the process assured Blake's success. In spite of her rationalizations, she was uneasy. Had she ruined a perfect relationship by tampering with fate?

He stalked toward her, looking like an angry golden lion. Even in her disquiet she admired him. As he came closer she noticed his rigid jaw, the small muscle that clenched in his cheek. She zipped her hooded parka and rose from her seat. She wanted to be standing when she faced Blake.

"How did it go?" she asked quietly.

He looked down at her, not answering. She had never seen his eyes look that way, like cold gray steel, but she didn't flinch. The silence stretched between them, vibrant with tension.

Finally he spoke. "Do you have to ask?"

"I'm interested, Blake. I care about your project." She reached out and touched his face. "And I love you."

Her touch always made him smile. But not today. Today he was remote and unapproachable. She studied his face as her hand rested there. She saw his mouth twitch, then harden. She saw the brief quicksilver flash in his eyes, and saw them change back to cold flint. And she was afraid. She was afraid she had made a terrible error in judgment, afraid she'd created a chasm that couldn't be bridged. She was afraid she'd lost him. Her hand dropped to her side.

"Let's go, Jessie."

He didn't touch her as they walked from the auditorium. Gone was that wonderful sense of joy, that close camaraderie. In its place was a pall of suspicion. They boarded The Joy Bus and rode back to the hotel. Every attempt Jessie made at light conversation was rebuffed by Blake.

He didn't speak until they were back in their hotel room. Tossing his coat on the bed, he turned to her.

"Tell me about it, Jessie."

"Be specific, Blake. What do you want me to talk about?"

"I recognized your Russian sable coat. There's no need to pretend."

"I'm not pretending. I'm trying to be adult. I'm trying to prevent this . . . this . . ."

"Tragedy."

Her chin came up in defiance. "If you want to call it that. I prefer to call it a misunderstanding."

"This is more than a matter of semantics."

"I know that. But it's certainly not the tragedy you make it."

She went to him and leaned her head on his chest. "Blake."

He took her arms and firmly set her aside. "It won't work, Jessie."

"It will," she said fiercely.

He rammed his clenched fists into his pockets. "Dammit, Jessie. Don't you know how much I want you? Right now I'm having to fight myself to keep from ripping those clothes off that beautiful body and taking you like a damned rutting stag."

The passion blazing in his eyes stunned her. Her knees went weak.

"Take me, Blake. I want it."

"No."

"Take me now. Before the anger festers. Before it drives us apart."

"It won't work, Jessie."

"It will. I'll make it work."

"I can't be bought with sex, no matter how good it is. Nor with money."

His words hit her like a physical blow. Her head came up and her green eyes glittered.

"Is that what we've had?" she asked. "Just sex?"

Pain struggled with his anger. "I didn't mean it that way."

"Well, how did you mean it, almighty psychology professor, friend of the underdog? Didn't you ever hear that charity begins at home? Where were all your noble ideals when you condemned me without a trial?" Her hurt spawned the bitter words. And once said, they couldn't be taken back.

Some of the anger drained out of Blake. He knew she spoke the truth. He'd convicted her without giving her a chance to explain. He, who prided himself on fairness, had condemned the woman he loved without so much as asking her why she had tampered with the bet. Love was not simple, he decided. It had almost made him forget who he was.

Taking his fists from his pockets, he sat down on the edge of the bed. "You're right. You deserve a fair hearing."

"A fair hearing. That makes me sound like a criminal."

"Dammit, Jessie. I'm trying. I'm trying to be fair. I'm trying to understand."

"It may be too late for that now. I feel rejected. Discarded like an old shoe."

He could have wept. Silently he cursed the fates, himself, the ghosts of her past. He felt a compelling urge to pull her down onto the bed and soothe their mutual pain with love. To forget the woman and the sable coat. To drown everything in a storm of passion. But he knew that would be wrong. Left alone, the suspicions would grow, driving a permanent wedge between them.

"Please, Jessie. I want to know what happened. I want to understand your motives."

She crossed to the other side of the room and sat stiffly on a chair.

"I did a charitable deed. You taught me that, Blake. I've watched you help people. I've experienced the warm glow that comes from helping others." She looked down at her folded hands as the pain of remembering almost overwhelmed her. The Joy Bus. The river. The shared laughter. The funny, wonderful people like Wanda Lou. Her chin came up. "We have a Wentworths in New Orleans. I gave Mrs. Dempling a job."

"And your Russian sable coat."

"Yes. I'd left it in the bus. Remember?"

His eyes blazed. Remember? How could he ever forget? he wondered. Jessie, naked on the sable coat, waiting for him at The Bluebird of Happiness. His heart hammered from him just thinking about it. They'd carelessly tossed the coat, damp from their lovesweat, into the bus when they left the motel.

He steeled himself against the emotions that almost catapulted him across the room.

"Why, Jessie?"

"She needed more than a job. She needed a coat."

"I don't dispute that. I'm glad you were in a position to help her."

"Are you? Even though I'm rich? Even though I can afford to give away a Russian sable?" The hurt still pressed like a thorn in her flesh.

"Yes." He sensed the shell she was building around herself, but felt helpless to stop it. His own feelings were still raw from the deal she had made, and he felt justified in his anger. "But you're not telling everything. What did you receive in exchange for all these kind deeds?"

"It seems you've already figured that out."

"Why, Jessie? Why did you feel it necessary to send that woman to me?"

"I wanted you to win."

"Dammit!" He rose and paced the floor, back and forth like an avenging golden god. Suddenly he whirled and faced her. "I wanted to win, too, but not like this. Paid gratitude is meaningless. This is not a game. I'm serious about my research. How do you know Mrs. Dempling wouldn't have come to express her gratitude without the sable coat? Didn't you have any faith in me? Didn't you think I'd see through that sham?"

She jumped up to face him. "Call me selfish, Blake, but don't call me faithless. Yes, I have faith in you, in your research. But wanting to be with you outweighed all other considerations. I wanted you to win. I wanted to come to your house, to be a part of your life at the university. I wanted to get to know the whole man, not just the magic man." She spread her hands wide in appeal. "I wanted to make damned sure that would happen. Don't you see? I couldn't take any chances. I've loved and lost before. At least, I thought it was love."

" 'What a tangled web we weave . . .' " he said softly as he looked at her across the chasm that separated them. "The bet's off, Jessie. Nobody wins."

Her back stiffened and she spoke carefully, as if she might break. "You're right. Nobody wins. I should have followed my original instincts. I should have stayed in my ivory tower."

He studied her still, closed face and felt hollow, used up. They seemed to have said all that could be said. For once in his life, he couldn't think rationally. He couldn't analyze the problem objectively and come up with a solution. Pride and pain got in the way.

"Let's go home," he said.

Her head shot up as she accepted defeat. "Fine. You don't know how relieved I'll be to sleep in a real bed and eat real food." It was a lie as well as a punch below the belt, but Jessie didn't care. At the moment, she was beyond caring about anything except getting back to Jackson as fast as she could. She opened her suitcase and flung clothes at it, not caring whether they hit or missed, not caring whether they were wadded and wrinkled. "As a matter of fact," she said without looking at Blake, "I'm taking a plane home. I don't think I can endure another moment on that dilapidated bus."

"I brought you to New Orleans and I'll take you home."

She glared at him. "A little male chauvinism? I'm a grown woman. I run a multimillion-dollar business. I certainly don't need a man, magic or otherwise, to see that I get home safely."

"Jessie—"

"There's nothing else to say, Blake." She picked up the phone and called the airport. Her voice was lifeless, like a poorly done recording, as she made arrangements to fly home. When she replaced the receiver she looked at Blake. She needed every resource she had to keep herself held together. "I'll send a porter for my bags. Good-bye, Blake." She left the room swiftly, without turning back.

He started after her, then changed his mind. It was too late, he decided. They had lacerated each other with words. They had escalated a small misunderstanding into a major rift that had torn the fabric of their relationship.

Resolutely, he turned back to his packing. Her suitcase was still open on the bed. He stood for a moment, bewitched by the silky tangle of her lingerie. Need ripped through him so strongly that he felt a wrenching in his groin. With a muttered oath, he slammed the suitcase shut and locked it. Then, forcing Jessie from his mind, he packed.

Jessie was thirty thousand feet in the air before the numbness left her. Reality flooded in behind the feeling. She gritted her teeth and gripped the seat until her knuckles turned white.

"Afraid of flying?" Her seatmate, a teenager with buckteeth and acne, asked.

"No." She turned her face to the window to discourage further conversation. She'd be damned if she'd cry, she told herself. It wasn't the end of the world. She was old enough to take a few licks and come back fighting. She didn't need to run away and hide in Europe the way she had after Rick. She'd simply made a bad choice. Her third. Not a very good track record. Well, it would be her last. No more blind trust in the opposite sex. No more yearnings of the flesh. Blake had given her enough loving to last a lifetime. Correction. Enough sex. It was just sex. She'd have to remember that. She'd created a dream world complete with a dream hero. The first winds of adversity had blown the dream away, turned it to ashes. She should have known it would happen. Hadn't she had enough experience to realize that dreams are too fragile to withstand the bright light of truth? The truth was money and power and commercialism. The truth was man, prideful and selfish and fallible. The truth wasn't pretty, but it provided insulation against pain. Right now, she needed that. Insulation. And hard work. Plenty of hard work.

As the plane touched down in Jackson, she decided to put Dr. Blake Montgomery and The Joy Bus behind her.

"To the office," she told Raymond, who was waiting for her at the airport.

Although it was pitch black dark, he didn't question her orders. "Glad to have you back, Miss Wentworth. Though I was surprised to get your call."

"Change of plans, Raymond."

The limousine smoothly whisked her to Wentworths.

"Shall I wait, Miss Wentworth?"

"No. I'll be late. I'll call you."

She took the executive elevator to her office. Her shoes tapped sharply on the floor, punctuating her march toward insulation, isolation, and forgetfulness. She shoved open her door, snapped on the light, and walked to her desk. Taking a set of files from the top drawer, she sat down and went to work.

"I won't look back," she said aloud. "I'll never look back again."

At four A.M., the lights were still burning in Jessie's ivory tower.

Ten

Blake left New Orleans and drove straight through to the university, stopping only once for gas and food. He wanted to reach the sanctuary of home as quickly as possible. He wanted to be so exhausted when he got there that he would do nothing except sleep.

He gripped the wheel, concentrating on the road, listening to the monotonous swish of tires against the pavement, pushing the old bus to the limits of its endurance. The animals were asleep; his research notes were neatly filed; the magic props were put away. Everything was restored to its proper order. And he was lonesome as hell.

He missed Jessie. He missed the cereal bowl she never seemed to remember to put away. He missed her bedroom shoes, a frivolous pair of high-heeled mules, that were always lying forgotten under the passenger seat. He missed her smile, her exotic green eyes, the way she tilted her head so that her hair swung out in a shining curtain, the delicate arch in her foot, the way she moved.

"Why, Jessie?" He didn't realize he had spoken aloud until Sandy barked. "Go back to sleep, girl. I'm just a lovesick fool talking to myself."

He hadn't meant to think about her. He hadn't meant to try to analyze their relationship, to figure out what had gone wrong, but he couldn't seem to help himself. He had always been a creature of habit, and habits die hard. Almost as hard as love. Was the love dead? he wondered. Had they given it a fatal blow in New Orleans? Could something so extraordinarily beautiful die because of one mistake? He didn't know. Right now, he was too empty to tell. There was a great void inside him where his heart used to be. He felt like a shell of a man with no emotions, no joy, no pain, just bones held together by skin and muscles.

Why had it happened? That was the big question. Why had Jessie bribed a woman to come forward and express her gratitude? And why had he reacted so strongly? He could only speculate about Jessie. From what he knew of her past, from the things she had told him in New Orleans, he deduced that she wanted to make certain she didn't lose him.

Didn't she have enough faith in their relationship to know that they didn't need a bet to keep them together? Didn't she know that, win or lose, she could have come to Oxford to be a part of his life? Apparently not. Somewhere along the line he had failed. He had thought their relationship was carefully built on mutual trust and admiration. He had thought the gap between their separate worlds was bridged. But at the first opportunity Jessie had fallen back on her old habit of relying on her money to fix everything. Instead of trusting her instincts, trusting him, trusting *them*, she had used her wealth to get what she wanted.

Was it possible that, after all, there was no way to reconcile their two worlds? Had he realized that in New Orleans? Was that why he had reacted so violently? Noble enough reasons to justify his anger. But was that all? Blake decided he was being too easy on himself. Pride, not nobility, was the root of his problem. His pride was hurt that Jessie hadn't come to him to discuss her feelings. His pride was hurt that she had gone behind his back, as if she had no confidence in him.

The truth haunted him all the way to Oxford. He parked the bus beside his modest cottage, unloaded the animals, and went inside. As bone tired as he was, however, he couldn't sleep. The memory of Jessie kept him walking the floor until dawn.

Everybody wondered what was the matter with Jessie. Since she had come back from that trip, she'd been a workaholic, a tyrant, hell on wheels. Raymond speculated with Alvin, who discussed it with the security guards, who talked about it with the gardener, who figured Mrs. Jones knew but he knew better than to ask her.

Nothing pleased Jessie. She found fault with every little thing, from the tilt of Alvin's cap to the cut of Raymond's coat to the way the security guards opened the gate. Her employees told each other that only their deep respect for Jessie kept them at Wentworth Manor. They congratulated themselves on their loyalty and swore their genuine love, and never once did they mention their exorbitant salaries.

Blake's colleagues wondered what was bothering him. He had cut his trip short and was holed up in his cottage, working on his book as if it were a life and death matter. They never saw him ambling about campus, as was his habit, stopping to admire the old buildings, pausing to chat with friends. He never called to invite them over for coffee and he refused all social invitations. He had become a hermit, leaving his home only long enough to get food. The brief glimpses they saw of him in the grocery store added fuel to the fires of speculation. Concerned friends commented on the tired lines etched around his eyes, the quality of sadness in his smile. But worst of all, he had given up his magic. He had turned down three invitations to do magic shows, he never pulled a silver dollar from anybody's ear, and it was rumored that his magic props were for sale. Everybody wondered what had happened to Blake.

"It's been two weeks, Jessie," Hunter said. "How much longer are you going to let this go on?" Hunter had flown in from Dallas and was sprawled on the couch in front of the fire.

Jessie was curled up in a wing chair. "I'm sure I don't know what you're talking about."

"That sounds like a line from a grade B movie."

"You should know. Grade B movies are your specialty."

"Don't change the subject. The subject is you and Blake. What in the hell went wrong?"

"Nothing."

"Nothing? For Pete's sake, Jessie. You're sitting there knitting. *Knitting*, for crying out loud. Talk to me, Jessie."

Ignoring him, she bent over her knitting and concentrated on removing a knot.

Hunter got up and inspected the garment over her shoulder. "What is that thing, anyhow? It looks like a saddle blanket."

"It's a sweater."

"For me?" He grinned at her.

"No. It's for . . . for Alvin. I've been mean to him. I've found fault with everything he's done to the Ferrari for the last two weeks." She held up the lopsided sweater. "I thought I'd make amends by giving him a homemade gift."

Hunter roared with laughter. "More than likely that gift will send him looking for another job."

"You need not snicker, Hunter. Just because nobody's ever given you a homemade sweater is no reason to laugh at this one. Some people appreciate hand-crafted gifts. Some people place more value on gifts of the heart than on expensive gifts. Why, some people—"

"Blake?"

"I didn't say that."

"You didn't have to. It's written all over your face."

She plowed the needles viciously into the sweater. "You should take a new course in face reading. Dr. Blake Montgomery's opinions and philosophies mean nothing to me."

"Since when?"

"New Orleans."

"Aha."

"What does that mean?"

"It means I knew something had happened, something specific to break up what you two had."

"What we had was nothing." She attacked another knot in the sweater with unnecessary vigor. "It was a pipe dream, a mistake, a gross error in judgment."

"I don't believe that."

"Why?"

"I know Blake and I know you."

"Maybe you know me, but you don't know him. Even I don't know him."

"I don't know what happened—don't want to know unless you want to tell me—but I do know this: Every man has clay feet. In moments of weakness we let those clay feet show. We do things we'd never have done otherwise. We say things we don't mean."

"Maybe we speak the truth. In New Orleans, Blake had the courage to stop what never should have been. I've accepted that and I won't look back." She bent over her work so Hunter wouldn't see the expression on her face and guess the real truth. She *did* look back, and the looking back hurt. She remembered the sun in Blake's hair, the way his eyes crinkled at the corners when he laughed, the way his face changed from tenderness to passion when they loved. And remembering, she doubted. She wondered if leaving Blake had been the right thing. She wondered if she had thrown away happiness in a moment of anger. But most of all, she wondered if their love would have survived if they had given it a chance.

Hunter reached over and took her hand. "Look at me, Jessie." He pushed the sweater aside and tilted up her chin. "This is your old friend. You don't have to pretend with me. I know you love the guy." As she started to protest, he put his hand over her lips. "Shh. No need to deny it. I saw the way it was between you two before you ever left Wentworth. I'd hoped the trip would give you a chance to discover love."

"And what do you know about love, Hunter?" Her question was quiet, not mocking.

"Maybe more than you realize." For a moment

he looked into the fire, his face naked with emotion. If Jessie hadn't been so wrapped up in her own troubles, she would have seen a blaze flicker to life in his black eyes. She would have noticed the brief smile, dreamy and nostalgic, as a memory as bright as a butterfly crossed his mind. But it was all gone before she noticed, and Hunter appeared to be his usual carefree self.

"Jessie, I want you to be happpy, and somehow I think this is your last chance."

She gave a short, mirthless laugh. "I may be getting long in the tooth, but I'm not that old."

"I'm not talking about age; I'm talking about opportunity. I don't think you'll ever meet anyone like Blake again."

"I should hope not." She thrust her chin out in defiance, then she thought of The Bluebird of Happiness motel. Her stubborn facade cracked like fine china, and a tear spiked her eyelashes. "I hope not," she added softly. "I don't think I could stand it."

Hunter pulled her out of the chair and sat down on the couch with her beside him. Putting his arm around her, he urged her head onto his shoulder.

"Remember that time we were in Gulf Shores and I was building a sand castle?" he asked.

She smiled. "A storm was coming."

"And I was scared and wanted to go back to the condo, but you wouldn't let me quit. You said people should always finish what they start, no matter what gets in their way."

"I was just a child."

"A precocious one." He rubbed her shoulder. "Did you finish what you started, Jessie?"

"I don't know. Maybe there's no way to finish it."

"You'll never know with Blake in Oxford and you here in Jackson. Both of you stubborn as bulls."

She punched his ribs playfully. "Some friend."

"Friends tell the truth."

"Blake said that once."

"Go to him, Jessie."

"Why? He's made no effort to come to me."

"He doesn't have a good friend like me telling him what to do. Besides that, he's probably just as scared as you are."

"I'm not afraid of the boogeyman."

Hunter laughed. "I know that, my intrepid friend, but I think you're afraid of love."

Jessie was silent.

"Go to him," Hunter urged. "I've never known you to be a quitter. Go to Oxford and get this thing straightened out. Finish that sand castle, Jessie."

She suddenly sat up and grinned at him. "By the way, how's our protégée?"

"Does that abrupt change of subject mean you've decided to go to Oxford?"

"Damn, you're pushy."

"Does it?"

"Maybe. Now tell me about Wanda Lou."

"Monique. She wants to be called Monique, remember?" He laughed. "I've had every miracle worker in Dallas coaching our girl. In spite of that, she still remains the same unforgettable Wanda Lou. You'll see for yourself tomorrow."

Jessie was in her office, leaning back in her chair, Wanda Lou's designs scattered across her desk. And she was smiling.

Wanda Lou had been talking for some time and

was still talking. ". . . and Hunter says to me—he's a real doll, you know—'Monique,' he says, 'I think you should try this one.' And I says to him, 'Hunter, my sweet—'don't you think that sounds right sophisticated? My sweet, just as natural as them . . . those movie stars—'Hunter, my sweet, I says, I got my own style, you know. And it don't . . . doesn't matter a hill of beans to me what Mr. Neiman and Mr. Marcus think is the latest style, I know what's the best for Monique.' " She twirled around to show off her finery. "How do you like it?"

Jessie looked at the hot pink sweater, the orange scarf, the wide orange belt riding low over a full, ankle-length turquoise wool skirt, the bright turquoise boots. "I like it," she said honestly. "You're right, Wanda Lou—"

"Monique."

"Monique. You do have your own style." She smiled at her latest dress designer. With her face made up by an Elizabeth Arden expert and her hair tamed by a Vidal Sassoon stylist, she was amazingly attractive. Even the outlandish combination of clothes added to her charm.

Jessie tapped the sheets of paper on her desk. "And your designs are sensational."

"I know it. And with that new office you set up for me, there's no tellin' what I'm liable to do. Why, I bet the Queen of England will be comin' over here for designs by Monique."

"I wouldn't be surprised. This thirties-style silk velvet with the rhinestone-studded lace yoke is one of the first ones I want made up. We'll introduce you in the fall season. We'll have a big show in Dallas, lots of press, a big party."

"And I want that nice magician to be there."

"I can't promise that."

Wanda Lou perched on the edge of Jessie's desk and looked closely at her. "What's the matter? Did you two split the sheet?"

"What?"

"Break up, kaput, go your separate ways. My, my, that'd be a pure D mistake. I noticed them . . . those looks he was givin' you. Like he could 'a eat you with a spoon."

Jessie's knees went weak at the image. "I'm afraid that's all over."

"How come? You don't look like it's all over. Your face got all mushy when I mentioned that magician."

Determined to put the conversation back on a business level, Jessie cleared her throat. "If you'll sit over there, Monique, we'll select the designs that will go in the fall showing."

Wanda Lou was not deterred. "Nothin's gonna change 'til you make it change." Her new skirt swirled around her legs as she moved gracefully to a chair. "Yessir, that's my philosophy. Nothin's gonna change 'til you make it change." She tossed her head and leaned forward. "Hand me that top design, Jessie. I think we should start off with it."

Blake decided that two and a half weeks was long enough to mourn a dead love affair. The time had come to take action. He reached for the phone to call Jessie, then pulled his hand back. She'd probably hang up as soon as she heard his voice, he decided. He would write a letter. That was the best thing to do. He'd put all his thoughts into a letter that she could read and think about at her leisure. There was less pressure to a letter.

He started and tore up five letters. None of them would do. They sounded stilted, formal. He wadded them into balls and lobbed them across the room toward the wastebasket. Some of them hit and some missed. At least picking them up off the floor would give him something constructive to do, he thought as he pushed back his chair. When he stood, the old springs gave a protesting squeak.

He discarded the letters, put on his parka, and whistled for Sandy. "Let's take a walk, girl. I have lots of thinking to do."

When he returned an hour later the red Ferrari was parked in his driveway, crosswise, blocking the exit. Jessie! he thought. His heart hammered so hard he could almost hear its pounding. Assuming a nonchalance he didn't feel, he forced himself to walk toward his cottage.

She slid from behind the wheel and stood in his driveway.

His gaze swept her from head to toe. He took in the sleek raven's wing hair, the eyes, slightly almond-shaped and sparkling, the white ermine framing her flushed face.

"Aren't you going to say hello?" she asked.

"Hello, Jessie."

"Is that all? Just, hello, Jessie?"

"What have you been doing?"

"Missing you."

Blake had to use superhuman control to keep from sweeping her into his arms. He wanted to bury his face in that black hair; he wanted to smell the fragrance of her; he wanted to feel the texture of her skin. But he stood still. He knew that burying their problem under passion would be a mistake.

"Come inside, Jessie. It's cold out here."

"Would you get my suitcase, Blake?"

"Your suitcase?"

"Yes. I'm keeping a promise to you, and I think it's going to take more than a few hours."

He grinned as he took her bag from the trunk. "You're blocking my driveway, you know."

"I thought you might try to escape. Besides, I'm paying you back for blocking mine. Remember?"

His voice softened. "I'll never forget, Jessie." Taking her elbow, he led her into his house.

She threw her white ermine casually across the back of a Boston rocker. She was wearing a peach silk blouse by Ralph Lauren and a matching wool skirt. Blake thought she looked like a delectable sherbet. She was so gloriously beautiful that everything in the room was shabby compared to her.

"Coffee?" he asked.

"No. I don't want you to leave the room." She looked at him as if she would never get her fill. "I'd forgotten . . ."

"Forgotten what, Jessie?"

"The color of your hair. It's like sunflowers in the summertime."

His muscles tensed as he remembered. He remembered the feel of her hands in his hair, the husky sound of her voice when she'd told him she loved his hair. Behind the memory was the pain.

"I'm glad you came back, Jessie. I didn't want things to end that way between us."

"How did you want them to end?"

"What we had deserved more dignity."

"Had?"

"Let's not quibble over semantics."

"No, let's not."

He stood abruptly. "Why don't we go out to eat? There are some really good restaurants in Oxford."

She laughed. "It's a good thing I blocked your

driveway. I think you really would have tried to escape."

"Seeing you is . . ." He let his voice trail off. "I think we should be in a neutral setting, talking about neutral subjects. I think the wounds we inflicted in New Orleans are still raw. We need time to readjust our thinking."

She stood and he helped her into her coat. "Sometimes I wish you weren't so damned logical," she said.

Pulling the collar close around her neck, he looked deep into her eyes. "So do I, Jessie. So do I."

Blake had thought he would feel safe sitting in a public place with a table separating him from Jessie, but he didn't. When her hand had brushed his over the egg rolls, he'd wanted to leap across the table and devour her. When she'd sipped her green tea, he'd been jealous of the teacup. For Pete's sake, he thought. Jealous of a teacup because it touched her lips and he couldn't. Or wouldn't. He didn't know which. He was so damned confused about separate backgrounds and separate philosophies and bridges built and bridges torn down that he didn't know which end was which.

"How was the weather on your drive up?" he asked. Talking about the weather seemed safer than talking about New Orleans.

"Fine." Jessie felt like strangling him. She wanted to talk about their relationship. She wanted to know whether he still loved her. She wanted to find out if there was still hope.

She put down her teacup. "I don't want to talk about the weather, Blake."

"Neither do I." He looked at her and a big knot formed in the pit of his stomach. Jessie, who was so gorgeous she could have had any man in the world. Jessie, who deserved a king. Jessie, who spent more on one outfit than he made in a year. What in the hell ever made him think he could bridge the gap between their worlds? What audacity to think that she could be seduced by magic and simplicity! Hell, no, he didn't want to talk about the weather. But he was scared, deep-down, gut-wrenching scared. He was afraid he'd lost her, and even if he got her back, he was afraid he couldn't keep her.

He took a bite of his mandarin beef and wondered when the chef had started substituting cardboard for meat. "I suspect the new legislative cuts will have quite an impact on education," he said.

"The cuts will probably put us back in the days of the one-room schoolhouse. Some people can't see the forest for the trees."

"They certainly can't. I doubt that a damned one of them—"

"I'm talking about you, Blake."

"Jessie, I'm purposely being obtuse."

"Why? I've come to Oxford to settle this matter between us, not to discuss the political climate of Mississippi."

"I know that." He took a fortifying sip of green tea, but it didn't help. "For a man who's spent his life analyzing human behavior, I seem to be having a hell of a time analyzing my own."

"Maybe it's time to stop analyzing and take action."

"I don't want to hurt you again, Jessie."

"I'm a big girl now. I can take it." She smiled. "Besides, you're worth the risk."

"You make being sensible very hard." He reached

across the table and took her hand. Turning it over, he lifted it to his lips and kissed the palm. "Don't you know how much I want you? Don't you know I could make a fool of myself by taking you right here under this red tablecloth?" He gently placed her hand back on the table. "I'm glad you came to me, Jessie. But this time I have to be very sure of my own motives."

She gave him a lopsided grin. "Do you think the new tax bill will pass?"

He laughed. "I'd almost forgotten how wonderful you are."

They stayed very late at the restaurant. Afterward Blake took her on a midnight tour of the university. He was postponing the inevitable as long as possible—Jessie sleeping under his roof.

But he couldn't drive around the campus forever. Eventually, he took her home.

"Well, Jessie." He took off her coat and held it stiffly in his arms, absently caressing the fur. He couldn't think of anything to say. He couldn't decide what to do.

She laughed. "Are you going to show me to the bedroom, or are you going to fondle my coat for the rest of the night?"

Grinning self-consciously, he hung her coat in the hall closet. "I have a spare bedroom. I'll take your bag."

She put a restraining hand on his arm. "Wait, Blake. First I want to give you something." She opened her suitcase and pulled out a bulky object. Holding it tightly against her chest, she looked up at him. "I know we come from different backgrounds, and I know our philosophies are different. But before you decide anything, I want to give you this." She held the object toward him. "It's a sweater I started for you on The Joy Bus. I almost gave it to Alvin because I was so mean to him, but it was always your sweater."

It hung limply from her hands, one sleeve longer than the other, the bottom lopsided, the seams put together crooked.

Blake thought it was the most beautiful sweater in the world. "I'll always treasure it, Jessie." He shook it out and held it up to his chest. "It looks like a perfect fit. How did you guess my chest size?"

"I didn't have to guess. I had firsthand information. Remember?"

His head whirled so with the remembering that he almost forgot about being logical. Jessie on the table with the neon *H* on her naked hip. Jessie sitting astride him in the tub, laughing through the soap bubbles. Jessie in the sunrise with the jazz of New Orleans drifting in the window.

"I remember," he said.

They faced each other across the lopsided sweater, two people yearning for each other but both afraid of making another mistake. This time it has to be perfect, Blake thought. This time it must be right, Jessie reasoned. And neither of them made a move.

When it seemed that the moment would go on forever, when it seemed that daybreak would catch them in the hall still longing for each other, Blake broke the spell.

"Thank you for the sweater, Jessie."

"You're welcome."

"Good night."

"Sweet dreams, Blake."

And they went to their separate beds.

But they didn't sleep. Jessie had never known

what the expression "whispered through the pines" meant until she spent the night in Blake's cottage. She lay awake in her bed, listening to the wind in the trees. It seemed to be telling mournful secrets. It seemed to be whispering of promises not kept and dreams not fulfilled. The winter wind, soughing around the eaves, told of emptiness and lack of courage and love denied.

She sat up in bed and pushed the covers aside. The central heating unit in Blake's house was old and crotchety, providing heat only when it took a notion to do so. She shivered, but from more than the cold. She shivered from lonesomeness and love lost. She shivered from pent up passion and need denied. And she was determined to do something about it. She had come this far, she thought. She would go one step further.

Blake still loved her. She could see it in his eyes. She could sense it in the way he watched her. And that was all she needed to know. Nothing else mattered. Not New Orleans nor Wentworth Enterprises nor college professorships. They had love. Everything else would work out.

Without even bothering to get her robe and her slippers, she pushed open her bedroom door.

The wind in the trees had never bothered Blake, but tonight it made him restless. He rose from his bed and paced the floor. With his penchant for honesty, he realized it wasn't the wind that made him restless; it was Jessie. He didn't know how he could have sat across from her in the restaurant and talked about politics and the weather and taxes and the plight of education in Mississippi. He didn't know why he kept postponing the real issue—their relationship. What was holding him back? Dammit, he loved the woman. What was keeping him out of her bedroom? As he afraid of hurting Jessie as he had said, or was he more afraid of hurting himself? It wasn't a pretty question and he didn't much like the answer.

In the beginning he had set out to bridge a gap between their worlds, but in the end it seemed that he had wanted Jessie to abandon her world for his. What damned colossal ego had made him think she would turn away from everything she'd ever known and bow down to worship at his feet?

He stopped his pacing and picked up the sweater, the beloved, lopsided sweater that had shouted the answer he'd been too dumb to hear. Jessie was willing to compromise. She was willing to meet him halfway.

He buried his face in the sweater and almost laughed aloud. To think that he'd just about made the same mistake now that he'd made in New Orleans. The woman he loved was within his reach, and he'd almost lost her again because of false pride and faulty logic.

Too many precious moments had already been lost. He pulled on his pajama bottoms and bolted toward the door.

They collided in the hall. He gripped her shoulders.

"I have to talk to you, Jessie."

"I was coming to roust you out of bed, Blake. Why do you think I came to Oxford?"

"Why?"

"To keep my promise to you." She reached up and touched his face. "I promised never to let you forget that you love me. Remember?"

"Every moment of every day I've remembered. I've been a fool not to come to you."

He propelled her into the den and pulled her onto the sofa.

"You're cold," he said. He settled her against his shoulder and covered them with an afghan that had been draped across the back of the sofa. "Is that better?"

"It's better for warmth but dangerous for my state of mind. I can't seem to think straight when I'm this close to you."

"Nor can I. But it's just as well. I almost spoiled what we had with too much thinking."

"Almost, Blake?"

"Almost, but not quite. I've finally realized that what I feel for you can't be destroyed." He rubbed her face, his hands like a plea on her skin, pressing his case, communicating his need. "Forgive me, Jessie, for hurting you. The only excuse I have is that love is new to me. I don't yet know how to treat it."

She covered his hands with her own and held them against her cheeks. "And I almost destroyed us by superimposing the past on the present. I tried to protect myself, to make sure I wouldn't lose you. I tried to arrange fate." She swiveled in his arms and looked up at him. "But that's the way I am, aggressive and determined. I don't think I can change. Not even for you."

"Don't change, Jessie. I don't want you to change. The thing that's going to make our life together so exciting is that we're different."

She laughed. "I should hope so."

He reached under the afghan and rubbed her thigh. "Not that, you beloved idiot. Our backgrounds, our philosophies, our habits—" His breathing became harsh as his hand rediscovered the wonders of Jessie.

Twining her arms around his neck, she pulled

him so close that his mouth was only a thought away. "Blake, could you stop being logical and analytical for a little while?"

"For a long while, Jessie," he murmured as he lowered his mouth to hers. "For a long, long while."

Their coming together was forgiveness and healing and renewal. It was past and present and future. It was a promise.

Afterward, as she lay in his arms, he bent over and tucked a yellow rose into her dark hair.

"How did you do that, Blake?"

"Magic, Jessie."

Epilogue

"Are you sure this trick is going to work, Hunter?" Jessie asked. She was standing in the new children's department at Wentworths, adjusting her cape and top hat.

"Trust me," Hunter said. He had flown in from Dallas for the grand opening.

She laughed. "I did that once and look what it got me."

"A husband who adores you, a playhouse on the Millsaps campus— "

"I like living in a professor's cottage. It's cozy. And we still spend the weekend at Wentworth Manor."

Hunter continued as if he hadn't heard her. "—although, how Blake could leave all that pulchritude in Oxford for a Jackson university that's mostly *preachers*—"

"Still playing the womanizer, Hunter?"

He grinned. "The only woman who has come close to stopping me is Monique, but she's too busy with her career to bother with a pig hunter."

He handed Jessie a cane. "Did you hear her on the Donahue show?"

"When she called him ham and gravy?" They both burst out laughing.

"That's the only time I've ever seen him speechless," Hunter said.

Jessie looked out across the crowd that had gathered for the show. It seemed that half the city of Jackson had turned out for the grand opening of Wentworths children's department. But there was only one face she wanted to see. And suddenly he was there, blond and shining, towering head and shoulders above the rest. Her husband. Dr. Blake Montgomery.

She blew him a kiss as he made his way to the front. "We can start now, Hunter," she said.

She welcomed everybody, talked briefly about the new department, then entertained them with a few simple tricks she had learned from Blake.

"The last trick," she finally said, "is dedicated to my husband, who taught me about magic." She tapped her inverted top hat with the cane, then reached in and pulled out a rabbit. George wiggled his ears at the audience and waited for his pal, Floyd.

When the two rabbits were out of the hat, Blake, knowing the trick was over, started to clap. To his amazement, Jessie reached into the top hat one more time and pulled out a Chadwick baby doll. His mouth fell open as Jessie tenderly placed the doll in a cradle.

Smiling directly into his eyes, she reached into the hat again, and out came three more dolls in rapid succession. The audience applauded. Taking a deep bow, Jessie stepped down from the makeshift stage.

"You wanted four, didn't you, Blake?" she said when she reached her husband.

"Are you trying to tell me something, Jessie?"

"I'm not trying to. I just did. We're going to have a baby."

Oblivious of the crowd, he lifted her in his arms and spun around. "A boy. I'm going to have a boy."

"A girl," she corrected him.

Still spinning, Blake said, "I'll take him fishing and teach him to throw a ball."

"I'll teach her to read a financial statement and to ride a horse."

"He'll have dark hair like his mother."

"She'll be blond like her father." Jessie plopped the top hat onto Blake's head. "Let's go."

"Where?"

"The old pink bus is parked outside. There's one more trick I want you to teach me."

Blake set her down and turned to face the applauding crowd. He doffed the top hat and a dozen yellow roses fell through the air.

"How did you do that?" Jessie asked as he picked her up again.

"Magic," he said, and carried her toward The Joy Bus.

THE EDITOR'S CORNER

This summer is going to be one of the best ever! That's not a weather forecast, but a reading report. There will be some very special publishing events you can look forward to that reach just beyond the regular LOVESWEPT fare—which, of course, is as wonderful as always. Alas, I'm limited by space, so I have to try to restrain my urge to describe these books in loving detail. (How I regret that brevity is not one of my virtues!)

During the first week of next month, a brilliant and heartwarming love story will appear in your bookstores—**NEVER LEAVE ME** by Margaret Pemberton. (This Bantam book may be housed in romance sections of some stores, general fiction of others. Do look for it or ask your bookseller to pull a copy for you. Trust me, this is a story you will *not* want to miss!) British, a mother of five, and a wonderfully stylish and talented storyteller, Margaret was first published by us in December 1985. That novel, **GODDESS,** was the compelling love story of Valentina, a mysterious young woman who became a legendary film star, and Vidal, the passionate, powerful, unattainable man who was her discoverer and director. This story often comes hauntingly to my mind. Now, in **NEVER LEAVE ME**, Margaret tells the equally haunting, yet quite different story of Lisette de Valmy, of her forbidden love and a secret that very nearly shatters her happiness. The man she will marry, Greg Derring, is nothing short of marvelous . . . and the climax of the book is so full of emotional richness and poignancy that I dare you to finish the story dry-eyed.

The following month you have an enormous, happy surprise—the zany, chilling, sexy **HOT ICE** by Nora Roberts. I bet you've loved Nora's more than forty romances during the last few years as much as I have. (Yes, we do love books published by our honorable competitors!) How were we so lucky that we got to publish a Nora Roberts book? Well, because what she is writing for us is outside the range of her Silhouette love stories. **HOT ICE** is a romantic suspense, a zesty adventure tale with a grand love story between an ice cream heiress, Whitney, and a criminal—a real, non-garden variety thief with plenty of street smarts— Doug. They're the sassiest, most delightful couple I've encountered since *Romancing The Stone* and the first episode

(continued)

of *Moonlighting!* In the back of **HOT ICE** you'll get an excerpt of Nora's next romantic suspense novel, **SACRED SINS,** an absolutely breathtaking tale, which will be published in December, on sale the first week of November.

THE DELANEY DYNASTY LIVES ON! In July we will distribute a free sampler to tease you unmercifully about the marvelous trilogy **THE DELANEYS OF KILLAROO,** which gives you the love stories of three dynamite ladies of the Australian branch of the Delaney family. But we won't torment you long, because the full works go on sale in early August. Of course these fabulous books were written by the ladies of **THE SHAMROCK TRINITY:** Kay Hooper, Iris Johansen, and Fayrene Preston.

I must rush along now so that, hopefully, I can tantalize you with a few words on the LOVESWEPTs for next month.

NOT A MARRYING MAN by Barbara Boswell, LOVE-SWEPT #194, reintroduces you to a shameless rogue you met briefly before, Sterne Lipton. (Remember him? He's the brother of the heroine of **LANDSLIDE VICTORY.**) Well, Sterne has more than met his match in Brynn Cassidy. When she finds out he's wagered a bundle on getting her into bed, she sets out to teach the ruthless bachelor a ruthless lesson. But soon both of them are wildly, madly, completely in love with one another . . . and in deep hot water. Funny, touching, **NOT A MARRYING MAN** is one more superb love story from Barbara, whose work never fails to delight.

I can't tell you what a pleasure it was for me to work on Sara Orwig's witty and wonderful, **WIND WARNING,** LOVE-SWEPT #195. Savannah Carson and Mike Smith crash into one another on boats in Lake Superior. Mike quite literally falls overboard for the lovely lady, too, but grave danger denies them the freedom to stay together. **WIND WARNING** should carry a cautionary label—its heroine and hero just might steal your heart.

Never, ever has a tent in the wilderness held a more exciting couple than in Hertha Schulze's **SOLID GOLD PROSPECT,** LOVESWEPT #196. Heroine Nita Holiday is a woman with whom each of us can readily identify as we learned so well in Hertha's first LOVESWEPT, **BEFORE AND AFTER,** because she's an avid romance reader. Mr. Right seems to her to have stepped right off the page of a LOVESWEPT when she sets eyes on Matt Lamartine. And

(continued)

Matt can scarcely tear himself away from the beguiling woman whose background is so different from his own that it shakes him right down to his toes. From New York to Chicago to the vast, romantic wilderness of Canada, Nita and Matt pursue passion ... and the understanding that can make their love last forever. An utterly sensational romance.

As the New Year began some months ago I was thinking back over the years, remembering the writers with whom I've had long relationships. Among them, of course, is Sandra Brown whose warm friendship I have enjoyed as much as her superb professionalism. One of the many things I admire about Sandra is that she never rests on her laurels. She constantly challenges herself to achieve new writing goals— and all of us are the beneficiaries. In her next romance, **DEMON RUMM**, LOVESWEPT #197, you'll see another instance of how Sandra continues to expand her mastery of her craft for she writes this story exclusively from the hero's point-of-view. Rylan North is a famous, enigmatic, perfectionistic movie idol. Tapped to star as Demon Rumm, the late husband of the heroine, Kirsten, he moves into her house ... her life ... her very soul. Sultry and sensitive, this romance is one of Sandra's most memorable. A true keeper.

We hope you will be as excited as we are over the line-up of LOVESWEPTs and other novels that we've developed for a sensational summer of reading.

With every good wish,

Carolyn Nichols

Carolyn Nichols
   Editor
LOVESWEPT
Bantam Books, Inc.
666 Fifth Avenue
New York, NY 10103

LOVESWEPT

Love Stories you'll never forget by authors you'll always remember